A DOOM

WITH A

VIEW

book two of the goodnight mysteries series

elise sax

Copyright © 2018 by Elise Sax
All rights reserved.
ISBN: 978-1731470072
Published in the United States by 13 Lakes Publishing

Cover design: Elizabeth Mackey
Edited by: Novel Needs
Formatted by: Jesse Kimmel-Freeman

Printed in the United States of America

elisesax.com
elisesax@gmail.com
Newsletter: https://bit.ly/2PzAhRx
https://www.facebook.com/ei.sax.9
@theelisesax

For Sander
A wonderful cousin and a wonderful person…

ALSO BY ELISE SAX

PART 1: MATILDA GETS A LETTER FROM A DEAD GUY AND TAKES A TUMBLE

Local Businessman Offers Bounty for Rescued Giraffes
By Silas Miller

Local Businessman Rocco Humphrey has offered a $2000 bounty for every giraffe returned to him safe and sound. There are approximately three dozen giraffes running wild in the Goodnight area after they got loose two weeks ago during a parade through the Plaza.

"All of the giraffes are still in fine shape, no matter what the haters say. I mean, how would they know the giraffes are in trouble when they ran to the four corners and no one can find them?" Humphrey insisted. "But the Humane Society says we need to get them back pronto to the Giraffe Sanctuary in Boise, or Goodnight will have to pay a huge fine," he added.

Several giraffes were spotted in the Basin, but more than one of the tall creatures have wreaked havoc in town. "You can imagine what I thought when I woke up with a giant tongue in my face," a woman who wishes to remain anonymous said. "The damned thing had its head through my bedroom window and was going at me like I had sprouted leaves."

"They're everywhere, now," Doc Greenberg

complained. "Some towns have cockroaches. We have giraffes."

Goodnight grew to prominence after it hanged Daisy the Giraffe in 1882. Mr. Humphrey has wanted to reverse the black spot on the town's history with the Friends of Daisy the Giraffe Home for Abused Wildlife and the parade to honor the tall animals. Now, the so-called protected giraffes have run into the wilds of New Mexico, and authorities worry that they could suffer a worse fate than Daisy. Namely, the drought, coyotes, and bears could bring down more than one of these noble creatures.

The $2000 bounty will be paid by Humphrey on receipt for each giraffe that is returned to him unharmed. In cash. Humphrey can be found most days during work hours at the Friends of Daisy the Giraffe Home, and he eats lunch at the Goodnight Diner every day at 12:30.

CHAPTER 1

I crouched in my galoshes on the bank of the Snake River, looking for clues. It had been two long weeks since the body of the murdered girl had been found. The girl I had spoken to and who'd asked me for help. The girl who had already been dead at the time we spoke.

Yep, that's right. My name's Matilda Dare, and it seems that I can talk to dead people. And see them, too. I might also be able to bring the dead back to life, but that's another story. That realization had me a little freaked out, but I was calming myself down with the idea that there was a logical, scientific explanation for the whole thing. I had also watched *Interstellar* three times, and I figured that alternate universes and the manipulation of time and space could have just as easily

3

been responsible for me having entire conversations with a dead girl. I mean, she might not have been dead at all. She might have been flying around in another dimension with a robot and Matthew McConaughey. That would have explained everything.

But my new neighbors in Goodnight, New Mexico, were going with the theory that I could talk to dead people. Dead people sought me out and talked to me. That's what everyone believed now. Before, everyone thought I was crazy because my murdering, soon-to-be ex-husband had put me away in an institution, but now I was considered crazy with magical powers. I was the wacko witch.

It wasn't the best first impression of me, as I had recently moved into the town. But even though most of the citizens of Goodnight now shot me fearful glances as I passed, my newfound friends seemed perfectly fine with the idea that I spoke to a girl at my house, while she was lying dead in a ditch by the river.

"I'm so hungry. He won't let me eat much. And it's so cold. I'm trying to escape. He's strong. He likes to hurt me."

Her words haunted me ever since she had uttered them less than three weeks ago. A specter that had crossed over to get my help, and I couldn't give it to her. The guilt was almost as overwhelming as my need to solve the mystery of her murder.

Now, the dogs that I had inherited, along with a house and a newspaper, sniffed the ground near me by the river. "Find clues, Abbott and Costello," I urged the beagle and the black Labrador. I had been searching for anything to find out who the dead girl was and who was responsible for her death. But I had found nothing, and the Sheriff's department weren't any closer to solving the mystery. Her DNA and fingerprints weren't in any database.

Abbott, the beagle, shot his head up and howled, and Costello ducked behind my legs, making me fall butt-first on the muddy shore. "What's wrong?" I complained.

"Stick 'em up!" a man yelled, appearing above me on the hill. His arm was outstretched, and he was pointing something at me, clenched in his fist. Abbott howled again and ran away. Costello stayed firm, hiding behind me. I put my hands up. "Give me your valuables," he ordered.

"I don't have any valuables." It was the truth. My divorce was on-going and had cleaned me out. I had been eating mostly peanut butter and jelly sandwiches for the past week to save money. I did have a Nissan Altima with thirty months of payments left to go, but I'd rather he shoot me than give up my car.

"Throw me your purse," he ordered, gesturing with whatever he had in his hand. I squinted at him. I was blessed with fabulous eyesight, probably to make up for having no sense of direction and a complete inability to carry a tune.

"Hey, that's not a gun," I said.

My mugger flinched and slipped slightly on the hill. "It's not a potato, if that's what you think it is."

"A potato?" I was thinking it was some kind of high tech weapon, like a Taser Ball or a Mace Orb. Not a vegetable.

"It's *not* a potato," he insisted. "So, you better…"

He stopped talking and screamed instead, as a giraffe broke through the brush at a gallop. It sideswiped the potato mugger, who rolled down the hill, landing in a fetal position by my feet.

"He went that way!" a man yelled from the brush up above.

"Get the net ready!" another man yelled.

Two men trotted out of the brush, obviously running after the giraffe. One held a rope, and the other one dragged a net behind him. The mugger hopped up. He eyed the man and then looked at me, as if I had somehow materialized them as my defenders were armed only with nylon rope.

"Hurry up!" one of the men yelled. "Get the bastard or we'll never get that pickup, and we'll be walking for the rest of our lives."

"And the sports package on the satellite. Don't forget about that," the other man yelled back.

Bounty hunters. There were a million in town now that Rocco had issued a reward to get the giraffes back. In a depressed economy, two thousand dollars to herd a gentle, if giant, creature sounded like easy money. Yet, nobody had caught a giraffe so far. My attacker didn't seem to be up on the giraffe thing, because he obviously thought that the two men were running after him, instead of trying to make a living. He took off with his potato or whatever he was holding. The two other men didn't notice him and continued on, chasing after their new pickup and satellite sports package. I was alone again. The whole mugger, giraffe, bounty hunter experience was over. I sighed, loudly. It was pretty much a typical day for me since I had moved to Goodnight.

Abbott howled as he returned. He and Costello looked up at me expectantly. "You're kidding, right? You cowards. You ran off and hid while I was in danger. What's a dog for, anyway?"

As if to answer me, Costello licked my hand. Abbott danced around me, like there was no way I could reject his cuteness. He was right. I was a sucker for my two adopted dogs, no matter how much of a pain in the ass they were.

"Fine. I can understand that you didn't want to get shot, even if it was a potato. And it might not have been a potato. It could have been a Taser Ball. C'mon, let's get back home. I know you want your morning bone and nap."

I wanted a morning bone and nap, too, but as the new owner of the Goodnight Gazette, I had to get to work. Investigating the death of a strange girl wasn't part of my duties. The senior reporter Silas Miller was covering the story, and there hadn't been a new angle to it since the day the girl's body was discovered. My investigation, therefore, was a personal one and had to be undertaken on my own time.

"Back to the grindstone," I told my dogs, and we left the scene of the crime.

My house was located in the hills above the Plaza in the center of town. It was a rundown, historical home hundreds of years old, built as a one-story square with a courtyard in the middle. My living quarters were on the right, and the Goodnight Gazette was housed up front. The paper was part of my inheritance and was keeping my lights on and my belly full of peanut butter and jelly sandwiches. Not much else. I was learning the journalism game, but I still didn't know anything about running a paper. Thank goodness the managing editor, Klee Johnson, knew everything about it, and thank goodness Silas Miller wrote ninety percent of the articles. Nine percent were written by the fifteen-year-old paperboy, Jack Remington. He was some kind of reporting prodigy and shared the same sensibilities as his mentor, Silas, that journalism was holier than the Pope, and it was their patriotic duty to "stir things up" and take no prisoners. I wrote the other one percent of the articles.

"There you are," Klee said as I entered, not looking over from the spreadsheet on her monitor. "You know, being the boss doesn't mean you don't have to carry your weight."

"I was doing Gazette business," I lied, sort of. The dead girl case was a Gazette story, but it had been written already. There hadn't been any new developments since then. I dug two dog bones out of the cabinet in the little kitchen at the back of the office and tossed them to Abbott and Costello. The dogs wagged their tails in appreciation and galloped out of the office to find a place to chew and probably fall asleep for the next four hours.

Klee harrumphed. "I'll be the one to tell you what's a Gazette story. What's *your* story. That's my job, you know. Otherwise, it's complete chaos around here, and the paper will fold. Is that what you want?"

"No?" I said like a question. Klee was a very fashionable, formidable woman, and I was half-scared of her at all times. With the cooler weather, Klee was wearing a handwoven turquoise-colored scarf that wound three times around her neck. Her straight, thick black hair hung down to her waist, and a hand-crafted bronze earring peeked out from her dark tresses. Meanwhile, I was wearing shorts and a tank top. I had shrugged out of the galoshes for a pair of flip-flops.

My cardigan sweater was hanging on the back of my chair at my desk. I put it on and sat down. I jiggled the computer mouse to make the monitor come to life. There, I found my assignment from Klee, sent by the messaging system.

"Letters to the editor," I read. "We still get those?"

"Go through them and pick out three," Klee ordered. "I need them in an hour."

Before I started working at the paper, I had always envisioned the life of a journalist as a relaxing one. Long lunches, secret meetings in parking garages, that sort of thing. But Klee kept me on a short leash, maintaining an environment where I was always late and running to catch up.

It did make the day go by quickly, though, but I did find a gray hair this morning. It could have either been because of the tight deadlines or talking to a dead girl. Either one. It was a toss-up.

I opened the letters to the editor file. There were about fifteen waiting to be read. The first one was a complaint about New Sun Petroleum's demise and the loss of jobs. The letter writer singled me out as the cause of that, so I rejected that letter. I was tempted to write back and explain that New Sun had kidnapped me and tried to kill me, but I only had an hour to get through all of the letters, so I decided to take the Dalai Lama's route and let it pass.

The next letter was all about the giraffes, and it was written by Mabel Kessler, a local entrepreneur who worked tirelessly to breathe life into Goodnight and get it running again.

Rocco Humphrey moved into this town and turned it into a shambles, she wrote. *He should have left well enough alone with the damned giraffes. So we hanged a giraffe in the 1800s. Get over it, people! Now, I'm trying to bring in traffic with my Tea Party Raves, and I have to worry about getting trampled by giraffes. Not to mention the tabloid interest in this debacle! This is Richard Gere and the gerbil all over again. Rocco needs to answer for this. Do you hear that, Rocco? Round up those giraffes and move them on to Boise before you totally sink Goodnight. Capiche?*

It was a good letter. I put it in the keeper file and moved on. It turned out there were three more by Mabel, which I ignored and one by Rocco, defending his position. I read up until the point where he compared himself to Jesus and quoted the Magna Carta and then put it into the keeper file. One more to go. As assignments went, this one was pretty easy.

The next letter was pornographic, and another one was an advertisement for a heel buffer. That's when I got to the letter that started the whole nightmare and turned my week into a whirlwind of craziness and murder. It was written from a funky email address, and it only had three short sentences and a list of letters.

Help! A matter of life or death. Urgent!
SH
MM
TE
Best Regards, Leonard

My ears grew hot, and I sprouted goosebumps on my arms. It wasn't the first time that I had this response. I seemed to get the same physical reaction from all things mystery, like I was an addict or something.

I was about to alert Klee to the letter when a car door slammed outside, and I jumped a foot in the air off my chair. My hand flew to my hair, and I patted it into place and sucked in my stomach. Every car driving up to the house did the same thing to me since Boone had left. Not that I cared when he was going to come back, I tried to tell myself, but my body sure seemed to care, and it went into overdrive with the thought that perhaps he had returned. He was due to come back to Goodnight any day now, according to the note he left me two weeks ago.

Don't make any decisions while I'm away.

I knew what he was talking about, and it made me blush every time I thought about it. Make a decision about his brother Amos, he meant. Not that there was anything between Amos and me, either. Amos was still in love with his dead wife.

And besides all of that—the mysterious Boone and the mourning Amos—I was totally off men. Men were no good for me. I was still technically married to my murderer husband who had gaslighted me and put me away. Now he was bleeding me dry, fighting our divorce so that he could keep his inheritance money. Not that he was ever going to be released from prison.

Oh, God, please don't let him ever be released

from prison.

As for Boone, I didn't even know where he went. Mr. Mysterious. Mr. Dusty, practically homeless, living in the rundown section of my house. Mr. Five-percent body fat, washboard abs, physical perfection, all kinds of crazy chemistry hottie. So, obviously, he was no good, and I had no idea why my body reacted every time I thought I heard his pickup truck drive up to the house. And I also had no idea why I was now walking to the window, pretending that I was stretching my legs so that I could spy on the parking area at the front of the house.

Outside, there was no sign of Boone. Instead, the senior reporter, Silas Miller, was walking from his Chevy Cavalier toward the office. Silas was nothing like Boone. He was in his fifties, with more than his share of body fat, and he seemed to own only one suit. And of course, he had a job, while as far as I could tell, Boone didn't.

I skipped back to my chair as he walked in and flopped down at his desk. "What a goddamned day," he complained. "There's a maniac running around burgling houses, and you'll never guess what he's armed with."

Klee shook a handful of notes in the air. "I've been getting calls all day. I heard it's a zucchini, a rutabaga, and a baseball."

Silas ripped off his tie and threw it on a stack of paper on his desk. Then, he lit up a cigar. "That's close. A potato."

"Oh my God. I think he tried to rob me down at the river," I said. "I thought he was either holding a potato or a Taser Ball."

"What's a Taser Ball?"

I shrugged. "I'm not up on technology."

"I knew you were down at the river," Klee said, accusatorily. "Wasting valuable time on a dead story."

Silas's eyes twinkled under his thick, gray eyebrows. "Never say die when it comes to a story, Klee. Good girl, boss. I like your moxie. You're bound and determined to find the truth about that girl's murder. I like it. I like it a lot, boss."

Silas called me "boss" because technically I was the boss. I owned the place. But there was no question that I was the lowest man on the totem pole. I was going to have to prove myself for a long time to come before I really was the boss.

"Did you find anything new, boss?"

"No. The potato guy showed up and then got run off by a giraffe and two bounty hunters."

Klee snorted. "It's getting dangerous out there. Every guy with a rope is out, trying to make two grand.

Mark my words. This is going to end up in disaster."

Silas gestured at me with his cigar. "So get ready, boss. It's on us to report the facts, save democracy, and keep the people of Goodnight in the know. We've got the potato guy, the giraffes, the bounty hunters, and the Plaza repairs. That'll keep us busy for a while. I love journalism!"

I didn't want to break into Silas's reverie, but I needed his input about the mysterious letter. I chose the third letter to the editor and sent the file to Klee. With that done, I printed out the mystery letter and showed it to Silas.

"What do you think?" I asked.

"What the hell is this? Is this from Leonard Shetland?" Silas asked.

"Who's Leonard Shetland? It's signed Leonard, but I don't know his last name."

"Leonard Shetland was found dead in his house about ten minutes ago after he called 911. I heard it on the police scanner as I was coming up the driveway."

CHAPTER 2

Silas assigned me the Leonard Shetland story. "Who, what, where, why, and how, boss. Remember, that. This is probably a simple one for the obituary column. Leonard ate a lot of cheese. Got that?"

"Yep. Cheese," I answered, even though I had the strong suspicion that any death that was preceded by a letter to the editor asking for help saying it was a matter of life and death, probably was a little more complicated than a straight obituary and it probably had more to do with something more nefarious than cheddar.

I stuck my reporter's notebook into my purse and left in my Altima. Leonard lived only ten minutes away. By the time I got there, there were three Sheriff cars and an ambulance parked outside. Poor Leonard

Shetland was definitely dead.

Getting out of my car, a long shadow fell over me, and I looked up into the gorgeous, manly face of Sheriff Amos Goodnight. Much to my horror, I giggled. Amos and I had shared a moment on his couch, which had been cut short by his memories of his dead wife. But there was still a doozy of a chemical reaction happening between us. It was like electrolysis but in a good way.

Was it so bad that I might have had a crush on Amos's brother after our moment on the couch? Was that considered incest? Was I going to be arrested?

I shook my head, trying to clear my mind, and I reminded myself that I was off men. Totally off them. Like way off.

Amos's brown eyes twinkled in the sunlight, and I giggled again. This time, his face turned a light shade of red. That's the thing about chemical reactions. They go both ways.

"What're you doing here?" he asked, helping me out of my car.

"Covering Leonard Shetland's death," I said in my best Lois Lane voice. *That's right, Matilda. Be professional.* I took my reporter's notebook out of my purse and slapped at it to prove I was on the story.

Amos's face cleared of any residual blush, and he

studied me for a second. "Wait a minute. I know that look."

"What look?" I asked innocently, trying to focus on a fingernail.

"The look where you get into enormous amounts of trouble, and I have to save you."

"Name one time when that happened."

"Well…" he started, counting on his fingers. "There was the time you were zip-tied, and then there was the whole getting shot at while dressed as an alien time, and then…"

I waved my hands at him. "Oh, forget it. You win. I might get into trouble from time to time, but I can assure you that I'll never ever get into trouble, again, and I will certainly *never* need you to save me again."

"Oh, yeah?" he asked, softly, his eyebrow arching.

We locked eyes, and my throat closed, making me cough. My body temperature climbed a couple degrees. *Danger, Will Robinson*, I thought to myself. *Man still in love with his dead wife!* But my body refused to listen to my brain.

"You know, there's a reason why I call you Trouble," he continued, and I could feel my ovaries shoot into action, lobbing a couple eggs down my Fallopian tubes, ready for some Amos action. I needed to put the brakes on fast. I needed to cool things down. I needed to come up with something unattractive about Amos.

Here was one: His right earlobe was ever so slightly bigger than his left earlobe. I found that out when I sucked on it. That was right after he had kissed me, and my head exploded. Oh, geez. Even his unattractive qualities made me horny.

"It looks like Mr. Shetland had a heart attack," Amos said. "Would you like to talk to the paramedics? They should be coming out soon."

Paramedics were okay, but I wanted to give Leonard's house a good snooping. "Are they sure it's a heart attack?"

"Yes. Don't go searching for a story where there is none. With every lunatic in a five-hundred-mile radius chasing after giraffes, I don't think you need to make up any stories about poor Leonard Shetland."

The coroner's car drove up, and Amos went to meet him. While he was distracted, I snuck behind the house and walked in through the back door. Leonard lived in a small, two-story mid-century house. It looked like the carpet was original to the home, as well as the avocado-colored appliances.

I scanned the dining room for clues and then opened all of the drawers in the kitchen. I had no idea what I was looking for, but I wanted to get as much snooping done before the paramedics were finished with Leonard in his bedroom. Finding nothing out of the ordinary, except for an impressive *As Seen On TV* collection of gadgets, I tiptoed upstairs to Leonard's bedroom. It wasn't hard to find since there were only two bedrooms. There was his and another room dedicated to even more gadgets. I never knew there were so many gizmos devoted to "abs of steel."

I found Leonard dead on his bed. The paramedics were done with him and were putting away their gear. "Are you related to the deceased?" one of the paramedics asked me, as I hovered in the doorway. Gnawing on the inside of my cheek, I decided on what to say. Silas wouldn't have liked me to lie about my identity. And Amos wouldn't even want me anywhere near poor dead Leonard.

"Yes," I told the paramedic, deciding to lie, anyway. Sure, I was officially there as a journalist, but I had ulterior motives, too. Even if I wasn't entirely sure what they were, yet.

"I'm sorry for your loss," the paramedic said. "It seems that Mr. Shetland died of a coronary, but the coroner will give the official cause of death in about a week or so. Do you want to say goodbye?"

"I can do that?"

"Sure. Frank, let's give the loved one a moment of privacy."

Holy cow, some folks were really trusting. A wave of guilt washed over me, and I did my best to ignore it. After all, I wasn't there to mess things up. I was just there to find out why Leonard wrote the letter and if he was murdered or not and if so, who did it. Was that so bad? I didn't think it was, but still, I needed to do it fast before Amos returned with the coroner.

With the room quiet, it finally hit me that I was alone with a dead man. In the past, I had touched a dead woman and she came back to life. I wasn't totally convinced I had something to do with it, but I figured I owed it to Leonard to give it a shot and touch him. Also, it would be a lot easier to find out why he sent the letter if he just told me.

"Mr. Shetland? I'm Matilda Dare. I'm sorry you're dead. Would you mind if I touched you?" I sounded like a lunatic, but I also had experience talking to a dead person, so it wasn't totally out of the realm of possibility that he would reply.

But nope. Leonard stayed quiet, his mouth slightly ajar, his lips white, and his eyes open and staring at the ceiling. He was bald, and he had eczema on his scalp. He was still in his pajamas, but his shirt was open and the covers pulled off, probably because the paramedics had attempted to do CPR on him.

"Here I come," I warned him. I laid my hand on his arm and waited. Nothing. I watched his chest for a rise and fall, but Leonard Shetland was deader than a doornail. The sound of the front door opening downstairs traveled back to me, along with men talking. I didn't have a lot of time. Opening the nightstand drawer, I gathered a stack of papers and a small book and stuffed them into my purse. It was way more than snooping. It was definitely tampering, and both Silas and Amos would be furious with me if they found out. But I didn't return the papers.

I had graduated from a snooper to a tamperer. It was only a hop, skip, and a jump to robbing banks and kidnapping celebrities. I was so going to hell.

The door to the bedroom opened, and the coroner and his assistant walked in, pushing a gurney. Unfortunately, Amos was right behind them. He shot me a look that confirmed that I was a bad person. I shrugged.

"Are you related to the deceased?" the coroner asked. "I'm sorry for your loss."

"She's not related," Amos said. "She's with the press."

The coroner's expression changed from kindly old man to angry old man. "You're not allowed in here.

What were you doing to the body?"

"Nothing!" I said and crossed my fingers behind my back. People weren't real receptive to the bringing dead people back to life narrative.

"She's looking for clues," Amos supplied. He still wasn't smiling. That was pretty typical of Amos. No talking. No smiling. Just a big pile of testosterone topped with a cowboy hat.

"My report will be public in about a week," the coroner said and shooed me out of the room.

Amos walked me to my car. "I didn't do anything to him, and he didn't talk to me," I told him. Amos arched an eyebrow. "Well, it's not unheard of for a dead person to talk to me, you know. Anyway, can you answer some questions for my article?" Silas would kill me if I didn't return with the what, where, when, who, how, and why.

Amos tilted his cowboy hat back on his head, and he leaned forward, making me take a step backward until my back was up against my Nissan. "Are you free tomorrow night?" he asked, startling me.

"Am I what?"

"Can you make it to my house at around five tomorrow? I have to ask you something."

I had so many questions. First of all, I wanted to know what he had to ask me that had to wait until I was alone with him at night in his beautiful house, nestled in a million acres of romantic wilderness.

Second of all, what did he want to ask me? Did he want to ask me to be his? To bear his children and let him adore me for the rest of my life like he did with his wife? What? What? What did he want to ask me?

"I think I have an opening tomorrow," I said and blushed at the sexual innuendo.

"Thank you. It's important." He tipped his hat back low over his eyes and opened my car door for me. It wasn't until I had turned onto the next street that I realized I hadn't actually interviewed anybody, and I didn't have the start or end or middle of the story about Leonard's death.

"I'm so not Carl Bernstein," I complained to my reflection in the rearview mirror. "I need fried chicken. I can't eat one more peanut butter and jelly sandwich. I don't care if it's eleven dollars."

I parked in front of Goodnight Diner in the Plaza. The Plaza had been dinged up two weeks ago from the visiting crowds who had expected an alien invasion, the parade of giraffes, and a firefight. Rocco said he had volunteered to fix the damage with some spackle and a coat of paint, but I heard that the mayor had twisted his arm and threatened to rat him out to the IRS about his precious gem collection if he didn't fix the damage. Three workers had been going at the repairs for the past two weeks.

Goodnight Diner was doing bang-up business. Since New Sun Petroleum had closed, most of its employees had left the state in search of other work. I had assumed that the diner would have been more or less deserted because of it, but inside, it was packed to the rafters. Gone were the usual hard hats and uniforms, and in their place were the everyday folk of about half of the town. They were all there to eat lunch, and I didn't blame them. The diner served delicious family-style meals.

The owner of the diner was one of my new friends, Adele. She greeted me at the door. Her hair was escaping from her ponytail, and her eyes were wild and bloodshot. "Hello!" she croaked, loudly. "Find a seat, if you can. It's bedlam. Total bedlam. They just eat and eat and eat and eat. They're like cows with multiple stomachs or horses with a feedbag attached to their faces. They don't stop. It's a steady stream of never-ending eaters in here. It's like the Post Office except with dirty dishes and sticky tables. I'm about ready to kill each and every one of these good for nothing binge-eaters. Don't they ever stop eating?"

I thought about pointing out that eaters were good for diner business, but Adele didn't seem to be in the mood for logic. She was overwhelmed, and even though she was bringing in a fortune, she was fed up and needed a lot of sleep. And in her state, I wouldn't put it past her to stab me in the eye with a fork. So, I shut up and nodded a lot when she talked to me.

"Will one of you good-for-nothings stop chewing for two seconds and push over so that Matilda can sit down?" Adele called out. "I see you, Rocco Humphrey, over there taking a big booth all by yourself."

Rocco did his best to ignore her and not make eye contact with me. It was no secret that Rocco blamed me for the giraffe fiasco. He was convinced that if I had only agreed to ride a giraffe in the parade and not have started a shootout, then the giraffes would be safe, Goodnight's reputation would be saved, and he wouldn't be on the hook for two-thousand a giraffe and labeled the pariah of the town.

"Come over here," my friend Nora called from the corner of the diner. She was at a small table for two, sitting with three men, one of whom was standing. She punched one of the seated men in the arm. "Get up! Don't you see a lady needs to sit?" She yanked the chair out from under him, and he fell to the floor. He took his plate off the table and continued eating on the floor. "Come on, Matilda. I have something to tell you."

I weaved between tables and sat down across from Nora. "I'm sorry," I told the man, whose chair I had taken.

"No problem," he said with his mouth full. "I'm just glad I got to eat something."

"What's happening? What's going on? Why is everybody here?" I asked Nora.

"It's been like this since the tamale lady left. She was feeding most of the town with her burritos and tamales. Now she's gone, and folks are hungry. Her cousin Tito was taking up the slack with his carnitas truck, but it was too much for him, so he moved on to a town up north."

"What'll you have?" Adele asked me, showing up at the table. She swiped some sweaty hair off her face with the back of her hand.

"Fried chicken," I said.

"That sounds good," the man on the floor said.

"We're out of fried chicken," Adele said.

"Okay. I'll have the enchiladas," I said.

"That sounds good, too," the man on the floor said.

"Nope. We haven't seen a tortilla in three hours," Adele grumbled.

"Meatloaf?" Adele shook her head no. "A hamburger? Chef salad? BLT?" Nope. Nope. Nope.

They were out of everything.

"I'm eating a pimento omelet," the man standing next to me said and showed me his plate. Blech.

"How about French fries? You got any of that?" I asked Adele.

"I'll try to find you some. My cook Morris is having a nervous breakdown. I'm going to have to give him a raise at this rate."

"I have a Xanax in my purse you could give him," Nora offered. Adele put her hand out, and Nora dropped a little white pill in it.

"If he doesn't want it, I'll take it," Adele said and stomped back to the kitchen.

"How do I look?" Nora asked me. She fluffed her hair. Nora had thirteen children and worked full-time at the bank and never seemed overwhelmed or wrinkled.

"Great."

"What do you think of my outfit? Too banky?"

She was wearing a brown sweater and a long black skirt. "Not too banky? Did they change the dress code at the bank?"

"Huh? No! I'm not at the bank anymore. This morning Jenny and Joyce came in to make a deposit and told me they were looking for a new assistant.

They've got big bucks, Matilda. Not to mention a mansion with a gorgeous view. I figure I can bring at least three kids to work with me, and Jenny and Joyce will never even know they're there. I'll probably have to do some shopping and errands for them and not much else. So easy."

"You're starting today? What about the bank?"

"They haven't given me a raise in six years. When I got the job offer, I told the bank to shove it. Then, they had the nerve to offer me a one-percent raise. One-percent, Matilda! Meanwhile, Jenny and Joyce are doubling my salary. You know what that means?"

"What?" I asked.

"No more generic pasta. I'm going to buy the name brand kind."

"And name brand toilet paper?"

"I'm not Midas, Matilda," she said. "You know how many butts need wiping in my family?"

Adele tossed a plate on the table in front of me. "We were out of potatoes. So, Morris used rutabagas."

"What's a rutabaga?" I whispered to Nora when Adele walked away.

"I don't know, but it's twenty cents a pound at Goodnight Grocery."

Feeding so many mouths made Nora an expert

on food prices. I tasted a rutabaga fry. It was nothing like a French fry. It was hot, and that's where the similarities stopped. I could hear Adele in the kitchen, pleading with Morris the cook not to quit, so I decided not to re-order.

"How do I smell?" Nora asked me.

"I only smell rutabaga and that guy's pimento omelet."

"So no baby spit up? My youngest did some projectile stuff this morning that would have made Stephen King afraid."

The door to the diner opened, and Mabel stormed in. She stomped over to Rocco in her sensible green tennis shoes, clutching her large purse to her chest. Her lips were pressed together so much that they nearly disappeared into her mouth.

"You!" she shouted at him, pointing at his face. "You've ruined this town, and now you're ruining my business."

Rocco turned a dark shade of red, and he dropped his fork on his plate. "Mabel, you look very nice today. Did you get a new hairdo?"

"I've cut my own hair with nail scissors since I was fourteen," she said. "Don't try and distract me, Rocco Humphrey. What're you going to do about these giraffes?"

"It'll be handled soon, Mabel. I put a bounty on them. There's folks coming in from all over to make sure those giraffes are safe and sound."

"You're an ass, Rocco. A complete fool."

"Don't be like that, Mabel," he whined. If Rocco had been a dog, he would have been on his back. The normally egomaniacal man was completely submissive to Mabel.

The diner had turned quiet, and the crowd had put their lunches on hold while they listened to Mabel dress down Rocco.

"I'm going over your head," she growled at him. "I'm bringing in the big guns."

"No guns! Please no, Mabel," Rocco implored.

"Don't be stupid. I meant I'm bringing in someone competent. Not like you. In fact, I'm bringing in two people. Meeting at seven tomorrow evening at the rec center!" she announced loudly to the patrons and walked out. As soon as she left, the diner roared back to life.

"What was that about?" I asked Nora.

"Poor Rocco is so in love with Mabel."

I blinked. "Excuse me? What did you say?"

Nora leaned forward. "Rocco met Mabel at some kind of meeting in New York and fell instantly in love. He moved out here to woo her and make her his.

'Course she has no interest in him. In my humble opinion, she's not interested in anybody. She's married to her work."

It was hard to picture Mabel and Rocco together as a couple. First off, Mabel was six inches taller than Rocco. Second of all, I couldn't imagine Rocco as lovesick. He wasn't exactly a touchy-feely individual.

My stomach growled. It was going to be another peanut butter and jelly sandwich for me for lunch. I put a five-dollar bill down on the table for the rutabaga fries and Adele's trouble. "I guess I should go. I have a story to write."

"I really liked your last one about the repaving of the Goodnight UFOs parking lot," Nora told me.

"Thanks. It's harder than you think to write about asphalt."

"I bet. Has the dead girl shown up again?"

"No. I think she must be deader now. Like too dead to talk." Speaking of too dead to talk, I thought about Leonard Shetland and the mystery of his letter. "Hey, do you know a guy named Leonard Shetland?"

Nora's face brightened, and she smiled wide. "Sure. That's who I'm replacing at my new job. Jenny and Joyce said Leonard up and quit this morning."

CHAPTER 3

My internal friend-o-meter told me not to mention Leonard Shetland's demise to Nora. She had quit her job, and she was so happy about her new one that I couldn't bring myself to rain on her parade. She would find out soon enough about her predecessor's fate. Besides, it was completely possible that her new employers had nothing to do with Leonard's death. So, when Nora gave me a hug and left to start her new life as an assistant, I let her go with a "good luck," a "congratulations," and a hug. Even so, I promised myself to get to the bottom of Leonard's death as soon as possible and make sure that Nora was safe.

I drove home and parked next to Klee's Cadillac. There still no sign of Boone's truck. Walking past the Gazette's office, I turned right into the living quarter's section of the house. The home was hundreds of years old, and it looked like it. My friend Faye was a local contractor and had decided to redo my house in her spare time. I had been thrilled at first, but her latest efforts were delayed so that she could do another job, and now half of my house was in shambles. I sidestepped a large hole in the floor in my living room on my way to the kitchen. Abbott and Costello were sound asleep in the corner. I retrieved the jam and milk from the refrigerator and took them to the pantry to make my sandwich. After, I brought my sandwich, a glass of milk, and a box of Cheez-Its to the Gazette office.

"You get the story?" Silas asked me. He was eating at his desk, too. A corned beef sandwich and a pickle. I was dying for meat. Peanut butter wasn't cutting it anymore.

"Where'd you get corned beef?"

"Grocery store. I hope Adele gets the diner under control soon. I'm not a lunch bag kind of guy. I miss my burritos and tamales."

"I think the whole town does, too. Carne asada burrito. Yum." I took a bite of my sandwich and tried to pretend that it was a burrito, but my imagination wasn't that good. I took a deep breath before telling Silas that I didn't have the whole story about Leonard Shetland for the obituary yet, and I needed another day. Klee stopped typing, and Silas gave me his best disapproving uncle look.

"Normally, I would tell you to get back out there and wear through some of that shoe leather, but there's been another one. So, I'll have you go out there for that," Silas said.

"What do you mean, another one?"

He slapped a slip of paper onto my desk. "Stella Hernandez," I read.

"She died three days ago of the flu. The wake starts in an hour. She was the deputy sheriff's stepmother, so we need to do something special. You know, for the press-law enforcement relationship and all of that blah blah blah. You got a black dress? That's usually what they wear at these things. And the food should be good. Maybe you'll get that carne asada burrito you've been wanting. Here comes Jack. He wrote her obituary. You can ask him about her."

Silas waved at Jack when he walked in the door. "Don't you ever go to school?" Klee asked the fifteen-year-old paperboy.

"I went for the first half, but the fourth-period biology teacher has greasy hair," he said, taking a seat at the desk next to me.

"Jack understands the importance of the fourth

estate," Silas announced with his usual fervor. "No greasy-haired biology teacher can give Jack the education he gets from the watchdog journalism that the Gazette does better than anybody. What's more important? Dissecting a frog or seeking justice for our democracy?"

"Well, I'm not bailing him out if the truant police come to get him," Klee said.

"There ain't truant police in Goodnight. I checked," Jack said.

"Jack," Silas said, seriously. "I don't mind truancy, but using the word ain't has no place in the Free Press. Show Matilda your piece about Stella."

Jack got the newspaper with his obituary in it and handed it to me after grabbing a pickle off of Silas's plate. "She died of the flu. I didn't know that can happen. I got the flu last year and pitched four innings at my school's playoffs with a hundred-and-two fever. Anyway, Stella was seventy years old. Big family. You know she was Adam Beatman's stepmom, right? I think he liked her pretty okay. His mom died a couple years ago. You know all that, right?"

I scratched my cheek. "Actually, no. I just moved here, and I'm catching up."

"Oh, that's right. Well, Adam's a good guy, but Amos says he has a bad attitude. That means he doesn't like to work."

"Amos said that?" Jack was Amos and Boone's cousin, and I wondered if he had any inside information about Boone and when he was coming back.

Not that I cared or anything.

"Adam's a good cop, he said, but he'd rather be watching ESPN. Does that make sense?"

No. It didn't make sense to me at all. I hated sports. But I did love a good Netflix binge while eating a large bag of peanut M&Ms, although that was a once a week sort of thing and didn't compare to sticking my nose into everyone's business as a journalist. My new job was so much better than ten episodes of anything back to back.

"Sure. That makes sense," I said. "Does Boone agree with Amos about Adam?"

"Huh? Boone? He doesn't work with Adam. Boone hates the sheriff's department ever since, well, you know."

I didn't know, but my curiosity lay elsewhere. "Have you talked to Boone lately?"

"You know Boone. He goes dark when he's out there."

"Where?"

"You know. The boonies."

Sheesh. Talking to a teenager was like pulling

teeth.

"Who are these people?" he asked me, picking up the printout of Leonard's letter.

"What people?"

"The initials. SH MM TE."

I ripped the paper out of his hands. "The initials," I breathed. "They're initials. He sent initials. Initials! Initials! Initials!"

Jack took a step away from me, afraid. "I heard that you hid under LeBron James's bed and when he walked into the bedroom, you jumped out and climbed him like a tree while singing the entire original version of 'Rapper's Delight,'" he told me.

Not this again. The whole town thought I was crazy. "I'm not crazy. My husband pretended I was crazy. It was all part of his murder plot."

"What about talking to dead people?"

"That part's true. At least I think it is. It's sort of up in the air."

"Stella's dead, but she's not going to wait forever, you know, boss," Silas growled, interrupting us. "News doesn't happen on our schedule. News has a schedule of its own. If you're going to be a fundamental part of what makes this country great, then you need to snap to it."

I grabbed my purse and the rest of my sandwich.

"I'm on it."

Stella Hernandez had lived in a small two-story adobe house about five blocks outside of the Plaza. Her little driveway was packed with parked cars, and there were more double-parked along the street. I spotted Adam's Sheriff SUV about a half block down the street, parked in front of a fire hydrant.

I squeezed my Altima into a small spot on the corner and reviewed Jack's obituary on Stella. It wouldn't be good if I didn't remember her name when I interviewed the guests at the wake. Stella Hernandez. Why did that name sound familiar?

I smoothed out my sweater and chastised myself for forgetting to wear a black dress. But when I walked inside Stella's house, I was relieved to find I wasn't out of place. The guests were all wearing shorts and jeans and assorted t-shirts. Barry Manilow was singing about Mandy on a stereo, and Stella herself was lying in an open casket in the living room. She was wearing a New England Patriots jersey, tan slacks, an inordinate amount of makeup in all shades of red, and a wig that was askew on her head, covering one of her fake eyelashes, making it look like a caterpillar was getting eaten by William Shatner's hairpiece.

"Doesn't she look peaceful?" I clutched my chest and tried to catch my breath. For a moment, I had thought that Stella was talking to me. But she wasn't. It was a tiny little woman holding a plate of food who was engaging me in conversation.

"Yes. Peaceful. Did you know Stella?" I dug my reporter's notebook out of my purse and clicked my pen.

"I live next door. I told Stella not to get the flu shot. Those things actually give you the flu. It's a government plot. Like stop signs and tofu."

I nodded and took notes. "Tofu."

Adam Beatman approached and looked in the casket as if he was searching for something that he dropped in it. "She went fast. She didn't even sneeze."

"I'm sorry for your loss," I said.

"And she stopped at stop signs, too," the little lady added.

"I'm writing a short piece for the Gazette," I said to Adam. "Would you like to say something about your stepmother?"

"You should probably talk to my dad, Abel Beatman. He was the one married to her. I just had to suffer through her dinners of tuna pot pie and Velveeta ratatouille."

My stomach growled. I really needed to get

some good food in my system soon. I glanced over at the buffet table. It was piled high with casseroles, tortillas, carne asada, and various salads. My stomach growled, again.

"So she didn't change her name when she married your father?" I asked him, trying to focus on what I was there for.

"Nope. I guess at her age, it was too hard to change from Hernandez."

A little zing went through my brain and came out of my mouth, making me yelp. "Stella Hernandez," I said. "Stella Hernandez. Stella. Hernandez. *Stella. Hernandez.*"

"Yes. Are you having a stroke?"

"No…I…Is that? Why yes, it is." I walked away, pretending I saw someone. Standing with my back to the wake, I took Leonard's letter out of my purse and looked at his list of initials. The first set was SH. Stella Hernandez? I gasped. Leonard Shetland had sent the paper with a list of initials, and the first one was dead. Dead from the flu. Who died from the flu? I mean, yes, people died from the flu, but nobody I knew had ever died from the flu.

Very suspicious.

Sneaking a handful of pigs in blankets off the buffet table, I tiptoed out of the living room. While I chewed on the pastry-wrapped hotdogs, I found Stella's bedroom. It looked like Laura Ashley threw up all over it. There was a crazy amount of ruffles happening. The comforter, the curtains, even the dozen or so wedding photos on the walls were framed with lace ruffles. Her makeup and hair brushes were still on a small table, and other echoes of Stella's life littered all corners of the bedroom. One-half of the bed had been left unmade, and I figured that was Stella's husband's side.

I sat down on her side of the bed. The nightstand was stacked high with tchotchkes, a lamp, a pad of paper, and a book. *Fifty Shades of Grey*. I picked it up. She bookmarked it on page forty-two. But the bookmark wasn't a real bookmark. It was a gold ticket. "VIP Ticket to Heaven" was written on it, framed by blue angel wings.

"I've seen this before," I said. But I couldn't remember where I had seen it. Still, it was a little suspicious that she had a ticket to heaven and then went to heaven. I put the VIP ticket into my purse and opened the nightstand drawer. There was nothing out of the ordinary in it. I heard footsteps in the hallway, and I slipped out of the bedroom before someone could rightfully accuse me of invading Stella's privacy.

When I got back to the living room, I made a stop at the buffet table and piled my plate high with food. I mixed and mingled for a little while, asking each person I spoke with if they knew Leonard Shetland. Nobody did. But I did get a lot more information about Stella and some good quotes about how much they liked her and missed her.

With a stomach full of food and my reporter's notebook full of notes, I left the wake and walked outside. Just as I closed the door, a man came up the porch stairs but stopped when black goo fell from the sky and landed on his head like rain with a loud *splat* running down his face.

"What the hell?" he shouted and had a violent coughing fit when the black goo dripped into his open mouth.

"Are you okay?" I asked. He hacked and coughed and spit black goo all over the stairs. "What is that on your face?"

He wiped his mouth with his shirt. "How the hell do I know what it is?" he shouted at me. "It fell from the sky! A gallon of black slime fell on me from the sky!"

"Maybe it came from a really big bird with digestive issues."

He squinted at me. "You're the crazy woman, right? The one from California who stalked George Clooney until he ran away to Italy? You chased away an

American treasure."

"I never did that. I'm more of a Tom Hardy fan."

"Now black goo is falling from the sky," he continued. "A lot of weird things in this town, but that's the weirdest."

I nodded in agreement, just as a giraffe galloped past, over the front lawn and between the parked cars before it ran down the street and out of sight.

I finished the article on Stella's wake and handed it to Jack, who went through it with a red pen, as usual. Most of my articles were more or less rewritten by Silas or Jack, but they told me repeatedly that I was improving. With the paper put to bed, the office cleared out, and I opened another file on my computer.

I titled it "Leonard," and I filled it with all of my questions and things I wanted to investigate. I included his letter and the list of initials, the VIP Ticket to Heaven, and Nora's new job. It wasn't much, and nothing alone was suspicious at all, but for some reason, I couldn't let it go, a lot like I couldn't let go of the mystery of the dead girl who had come to visit me, asking for help.

I turned off the lights in the office and locked

the door. I peeked out past the front gate to see if Boone's truck was there, but it wasn't. The dirt parking area was empty except for Silas's Cavalier and my Altima. Where was Boone? He should have come back by now. Not that I cared.

Although, it sure seemed that I cared. I was on the verge of being obsessive. Meanwhile, Amos had invited me to his house tomorrow, and I wasn't thinking about that at all. My thoughts only went back to Boone and the letter he had left me before he went on his mystery trip.

Maybe I had a thing for letters, and my interest had nothing to do with Boone. Sure. Let's go with that.

Before I walked into my living quarters, I peeked in the windows of Boone's part of the house. He was leasing it for a year, and I had originally mistaken it for a condemned storage area, but he was living there. He had left the door and windows locked while he was away, and until then, I hadn't broken in, despite my curiosity. Boone was still a mystery to me. I knew he was Amos's brother and Jack's cousin, but beyond that, I was clueless.

Standing there, trying to see through the window as the sun went down, I was sorely tempted to pretend that I smelled gas and break the window with a rock so that I could invade his privacy, but the sound of water running in my bathroom on my side of the house distracted me. I crossed the courtyard and walked into the kitchen. I fed the dogs and looked in the refrigerator to see if something had magically grown in there. Really, I shouldn't have been hungry after the wake, but the New Mexico mountain air gave me a perpetual appetite.

The water in the bathroom turned off, and I closed the refrigerator. "Silas? Are you decent?" I called.

"Sure am, boss."

I walked into the bathroom, and he was lying in the bathtub—thankfully covered with bubbles—reading *Foreign Affairs* magazine.

"Don't you have a bathtub in your house? You're here every night," I said.

"You should be glad your senior reporter practices good hygiene."

I didn't point out that he wore the same suit every day, and I wasn't sure how often he cleaned it.

"You're later than usual," I said.

"This is my second bath. I took the first one and went to leave, and black goo fell from the sky and fell on my head."

I gasped. "The same thing happened to a guy at the wake. I saw it happen. What do you think it is?"

"It smells like my crap after I eat the chicken

fried steak at the diner."

"That's not good."

"I kept a sample and am going to drop it off at the hospital's lab to see what it is."

"Smart," I said, impressed.

"Remember in a small town, everything's a story, boss. And if shit's falling from the sky, that's a headline that sells papers."

Selling papers sounded good to me. I was hungry.

"So, about Leonard," I started and gave him the full story, or as much as I had so far. "What do you think?"

"I think any ordinary editor would tell you to put your head down and report the stories we already have, not search out half-baked theories that have no basis in reality."

My head dropped in disappointment.

Silas slapped the water. "But I'm not any ordinary editor!" he yelled. "I'm a hard-bitten, take no prisoners, never say die, Edward R. Murrow was a god kind of journalist! Do you hear me, boss?"

"Yes, you're speaking very loud."

"Do you understand me, boss?"

No, I had no idea what he was talking about. "Yes. You mean…"

"I mean go with the story. Follow it wherever it leads. Dig deep. Ask hard questions. I know you're like a dog with a bone. I know you're still trying to find out about that dead girl."

"Well…"

Silas waved his arm, making the bubbles move enough to give me more of a view of his doughy body than I wanted. "Don't need to make excuses, boss. I approve. That dead girl is the most exciting thing that has ever happened in this town."

"More than the giraffes and the aliens?"

"There's a murderer out there who killed a young girl, and we don't have a clue about who that girl is. Never mind that you talked to her when she was dead. That's bigger than wild giraffes and aliens."

I nodded. I agreed. The girl haunted my dreams. I had let her down, and I didn't want to do that with Leonard. "So, continue with this story," he continued. "But don't let the other stories drop. Tomorrow you have to cover Mabel's tea party raves and I'll need you with me at the meeting about the giraffes. That's definitely a two-reporter story."

Whoa. That was a lot of stories I had to cover.

"Journalism never sleeps, boss," Silas told me, reading my mind. "You can do it. You might want to start early tomorrow and visit Nora at her new job."

"At Jenny and Joyce's."

"Or as most of us in Goodnight call them, 'the witches.'"

"Oh, they're not nice?"

"No, they're nice enough. They're just witches."

CHAPTER 4

The next morning, after I fed and walked the dogs, I made myself a cup of coffee to go and headed out to Jenny and Joyce Johnson's house at eight o'clock. I warned Nora ahead of time that I was going to visit her, and she seemed delighted.

"We'll have coffee and Danish, Matilda. Oh, you should see the place!" Her hours were six-to-three, which worked out well with her kids. "I've got two snuck away in their library. They'll never know."

Jenny and Joyce lived not far away from me, further up into the mountains. I turned off the road through wide wrought-iron gates and up a windy gravel path further into the mountains until I finally found their house. Their mansion. Their house was old like mine, but that's where the similarities ended. Their house was stunning. Gorgeous. Majestic.

I parked out front and rang the doorbell. Nora answered, opening the two-story Spanish-inspired mammoth-size door. "Look at me! I've got a new job!" she announced and gave me a warm hug. "Jenny and Joyce are giving me an hour off to have breakfast with you. They say it's karmically important for us to have tea together. Don't worry. I made coffee, instead. Who the hell drinks tea?"

The house that was a mansion was actually a castle. There was room after room of wood-paneled walls and antique furniture. "What the hell?" I said, gobsmacked by the opulence.

"Isn't it something? I'm telling you, Matilda, richer or poorer, it's better to have money."

We ate Danish and drank coffee in the kitchen, which was about the size of a football field. Halfway through my first cup of coffee, I was surprised to see Faye walk in. She was wearing her usual uniform of work boots, short-short cutoffs, a tight t-shirt, and a large tool belt.

She was sheepish when she saw me and when she plopped down on a chair next to me, she launched into apologies. "I'm so sorry, Matilda. I know I've left you in the lurch, but Jenny and Joyce were in a rush, and it's a really good job."

I put my hand on hers. "Faye, I'm not even paying you. Don't worry about it."

It was true. I wasn't paying her. She had decided to renovate my house because it was historical, and she enjoyed doing it. But I did wish there wasn't a large hole in my living room floor.

Faye leaned toward me and whispered in my ear. "I'm collecting all kinds of odds and ends they don't need. Your house is going to be amazing."

There was no better friend than a friend who was willing to do morally questionable things for you. She picked up a Danish and took a bite.

"Did you hear about what happened to Leonard Shetland?" Nora asked me.

I nodded. "He died yesterday. I saw him."

Faye sucked air. "Did he talk to you?"

"No. I went to his house for a story. He was just normal dead. You know, not talking or anything."

"Isn't it something that he quit his job right before he died?" Nora asked. I took a sip of my coffee and looked away. What was I going to say? That maybe her new employers killed him?

"He ate a lot of cheese," a woman with long, flowing gray hair said, entering the kitchen. She was accompanied by another woman with the same kind of hair, who was obviously her sister. They both wore gorgeous, colorful, handwoven clothes that were typical of Santa Fe.

"I'm Jenny," the woman said, extending her hand to me. Every finger was covered in rings. I shook her hand.

"This is my friend, Matilda," Nora said.

Jenny closed her eyes and took in a deep breath. She put her hand up, as if she was determining which way the wind was blowing. "Matilda is one of us," she said in a lower voice. "A kindred spirit."

"A sister of the psychic sisterhood," the woman who had to be Joyce said with her eyes closed, too.

"Really?" Nora asked. "So cool."

"Matilda talks to dead people," Faye said.

Jenny and Joyce flanked me on either side like a hippie sandwich. "We knew it," Jenny said.

"Your atomic aura filled the house the moment you rang the doorbell," Joyce agreed.

"Are you sure? I don't think I have an atomic aura," I said, growing uncomfortable with their attention. They were standing *very* close to me. Jenny's breath was peanut butter and peppermint, while Joyce was all about the cigarettes. They didn't seem like killers, but they were pretty creepy.

"Have you shown Matilda the house?" Joyce asked.

"We must show Matilda the house," Jenny said.

"She must *feel* the spirits of the dwelling," Joyce agreed.

"And know."

"Yes. And know."

"Jenny and Joyce are psychics. Did you know that?" Nora asked me. I caught Faye rolling her eyes at her coffee cup. Her husband ran a shop in town, catering to alien enthusiasts. She was a firm believer in the Vegan intergalactic army, but she obviously didn't cotton to psychics. I didn't either. That is until I met one back in Cannes, California. Now I was a believer, but I wasn't so sure I believed in Jenny and Joyce. They were more *woo-woo* than the psychics I had known.

Faye went back to remodeling the house, and Nora and I followed Jenny and Joyce as they took me on a tour of the castle. There must have been fifteen bedrooms. A maze of hallways, nooks, and passageways connected the rooms. But I noticed that the place was rundown in spots, the edges worn, and the rugs frayed. I assumed that it was a lot of upkeep to maintain a castle, and I worried that Faye would never finish with it and get around to fixing the hole in my living room floor. I could handle having a house falling down around my ears, but I didn't want to fall down, too.

"Why did Leonard quit?" I asked as they walked

me through the den.

"We don't know," Jenny said. "Perhaps he felt the universe call to him?"

"Yes, maybe he knew it was his time," Joyce said. "His soul is now traveling the cosmos. We're very happy to have Nora with us. She's already greatly improved the organization of our calendar."

"I hooked them up to Google," Nora explained. "Jenny and Joyce do a lot of readings, you know. People come to them for all kinds of insights. They told me that I was done having kids. Thank goodness. I'm so relieved that I might even let my husband touch me again."

"And now our readings are organized with the wonderful new calendar," Joyce told me, beaming. "Google means computer, you know."

I nodded. If Jenny and Joyce were on the up and up, perhaps they could help me about the dead girl. Maybe they could summon her and ask her more questions. As much as I wanted help, though, I resisted talking to them about the girl. Leonard's death was still suspicious in my mind, and I wasn't ready to trust the sisters.

We entered a great room, and I stopped in my tracks. My breath was completely taken away. The room was two stories tall with beams crossing the ceiling. The walls were covered with built-in bookshelves, and the furniture looked like it had been taken from Hearst Castle. But that wasn't the part that took my breath away.

It was the view.

The view of the century. The view to end all views. An entire wall was made of glass and through it was the view of a large canyon, forest, and endless sky.

"It's through nature that we know God," Jenny said.

"Would you like to go outside to get a better view?" Joyce asked.

She opened the door, and we went out back. The view was spectacular. The house was situated on a ridge, and far below us was a narrow, meandering river that ran through the canyon. Other houses dotted the land along the ridge all the way around the canyon. Even though the other houses were large and beautiful, they couldn't compare to Jenny and Joyce's.

"At night, the stars light up the sky, of course," Jenny said.

"So close you can almost touch them," said Joyce.

The sisters spoke with Nora about a yucca plant that was growing dangerously close to the house, and while they were busy, I continued looking out at the view. That's when I saw her. At least I was pretty sure it was a her. She wasn't far away, on the ridge. I wasn't sure what house she had come from, but she definitely came from one of them.

But now she was falling.

I pointed. "Oh my God!" I breathed. I watched as the woman rolled down the side of the cliff, hitting rocks and dirt as she went, gaining momentum and then slowing down and then gaining momentum again. "That poor woman!" I shouted.

Nora and the sisters turned around to see what was wrong. "A woman is falling down the canyon. Someone get help!" I yelled. But by then the woman had reached the bottom and was hidden by brush.

"Are you sure?" Joyce asked. "Maybe it was a coyote."

"Or a deer," Jenny said.

"Why don't you believe me? A woman needs our help. Call 9-1-1." I had left my purse on the kitchen table and nobody else had their phone with them. A terrifying dread crept up my back. I looked over the edge of the ridge. "She couldn't have fallen," I said.

"What did you say?" Nora asked.

"She had to be pushed. Nobody could fall from here. If it was that dangerous, there would be back fences, but look, there's not a fence to be seen. She had to be pushed. Nobody could fall from here."

Okay. So, I'm stupid. I'm highly educated in useless information, but I'm in no way a member of Mensa. I'm dumb. I should never open my mouth. That's what I was thinking as the ground gave way beneath my feet, and I started to fall down the side of the mountain to my death.

It wasn't the way I wanted to die. I wanted to die from old age in my bed after eating ice cream. I hadn't had ice cream in weeks. Why had I been depriving myself of ice cream? Now I was going to die without it. To think that I hadn't allowed myself to have a pathetic, fucking scoop of vanilla, and now I was going to die!

A lot more regrets flooded my mind in the split second between standing on solid ground and falling to my demise. But a couple of seconds later I realized that miraculously, I was managing to stay upright as I slid down, down, down. I was like a downhill racer but in sneakers. Putting my arms out by my sides, I started to believe that I was going to make it. I was the queen of balance. I was the Cirque du Soleil of the clumsy set.

"Look at me! I'm doing it!" I shouted about halfway down, and that's when I lost control, or rather, that's when my dumb luck left me. My ankle turned, and I went down. I slid on my butt for a minute and then I started to roll.

I rolled a lot.

That's when the regrets filled my head again, and I really wanted ice cream. And not to die.

And then finally it was over. I landed at the bottom. And miraculously, I was alive. I touched my body all over. There didn't seem to be any bones protruding. I wiggled my toes and turned my head. Everything was in order. I looked above me and could just make out Nora peering over the side with a look of horror on her face. I gave her the okay sign with my thumb and index finger.

My elation dulled when I noticed that I had landed a stone's throw away from the woman who hadn't been as lucky as I was. I crawled toward her and checked her pulse, even though I could already tell that she was dead. She was an older lady, and her body was banged up from the fall. "You poor lady," I said.

"Help me."

I jumped backward as if I had been pulled by a rope. "Did you say something?" I asked the dead woman.

"Please help me."

"Oh, no. It's happening again."

"He hurts me. I want my mother. I shouldn't have run away."

The sound wasn't coming from the dead woman in front of me. I turned around. A girl was standing there, barefoot, her long blond hair dirty, her eyes dark hollow orbs. She looked like she was a couple years younger than the other dead girl who had visited me. And I was pretty sure this girl had suffered the same fate as her.

"Who's hurting you? Does he have you locked up? Tell me, so I can help you," I urged her.

"I'm not the only one here. Blondes. He collects blondes." She stepped forward. "He's closer than you think." She touched my shoulder, and everything went black.

I didn't know how long I was out, but when I came to, Amos was hovering over me, and there was a lot of activity around me. "There she is," he said. He had taken off his cowboy hat. "You took quite a tumble. Don't move. I've got men here who're going to check you out."

"Is she still here?"

"The lady? Margaret Marshall. The meanest bitch in Goodnight. Although, she was always nice to me. Yes, she took a tumble, too, but she's much worse for wear."

"No. Not her. The girl. Oh my God, the girl." I sat up too quickly, and I got dizzy. The coroner was going over the older woman, and the paramedics were getting ready to examine me, but there was no sign of the girl.

"What girl? The dead girl?" Amos asked, cocking his head to the side, as if I had lost all of my marbles during the fall. Maybe he was right. Maybe I was seeing things. I really didn't want to be known as the crazy girl forever. Ditto the girl that spoke to dead people.

"No. Nobody. Nothing," I murmured and lay back down.

It took them over two hours to tell me that I was fine and that Margaret Marshall had fallen to her death. They put Margaret in the back of the coroner's vehicle, and Amos helped me into his SUV when I refused to go to the hospital.

"Holy crap, I have to get to a story," I said, as he clicked my seat belt on for me.

"Maybe you should take the rest of the day off."

"I'm fine." I looked at my naked wrist. "Look at the time. I'm going to be late."

"Where do you need to go? I'll take you."

"My car is back at the witches' castle," I said and slumped exhausted against the window. Amos started the car and drove it ever so slowly through the canyon.

"Are you sure you don't want to go to the hospital? Just to get checked out? You might have a concussion."

"Nah, I've had much worse falls than this." That was a total lie. I just fell down the Grand Canyon and lived to tell. I should have been dead, and that had me freaked out. Amos stopped the car and took a blanket from the backseat and draped it over me.

"You're in shock. Open the glove compartment."

I did. Inside were two handguns and a flask. "You either want me to put myself out of my misery or take a nip."

"I want you to take a big nip. It'll help right your system."

"Right my system," I mumbled and took a big nip. Then, I took a bigger one. He was right about righting my system. The warmth of the booze ran through my body, fixing me up until I was almost back in my right mind and okay with the fact that I had almost died like poor Margaret.

And then there was the dead girl who had talked to me. Dead girl number two. That freaked me out, too.

I took another big nip.

"There you go," Amos said. "You got some

color back in your face, and your eyes aren't doing that thing anymore."

"They were doing a thing?"

"A little bit."

"You know, I've seen the coroner twice in twenty-four hours. Old people are dropping like flies."

"Welcome to my world," Amos said, maneuvering around a large rock. The floor of the canyon was beautiful. Wild and lush with a river running through it.

"One heart attack, one flu, and one fell off a cliff. Three dead in two days," I said.

"Stella died before that. About five days ago, I think."

"Did the three have anything in common?"

"Yes. They lived in Goodnight. Here we are."

We had finally arrived at the paved road. Amos took a sharp left and drove like a maniac back to Jenny and Joyce's house. When we got there, I opened my door. "Don't forget tonight at five. My place," he said.

"That's right. It's Tuesday."

"I have something I need to ask you."

I got out of the car and closed the door. Nora burst out of the mansion with two toddlers in her arms and ran to me. Jenny, Joyce, and Faye were behind her. When she got to me, she put her kids down and wrapped me in a bear hug.

"I thought you were dead for sure," she said.

"Amos has something he needs to ask me at his house," I told her.

"No way," Nora breathed. She pulled Faye into our hug, and she handed me my purse. "Faye, Amos wants to ask Matilda something."

"Oh my God," Faye exclaimed. "You bagged the most eligible man in New Mexico. It's a good thing you didn't die when you fell."

I arrived early at Mabel's tea party rave. I had decided to take a lunch break first at the diner, but the line was out the door, and I could hear Adele screaming at people to stop eating. So, I skipped lunch and drove to the Goodnight Senior Home and waited around in my car in the parking lot. I played a word search game on my phone for a while and then went into the Senior Home a half hour early.

Mabel was in the lobby, ordering employees around. She spotted me and waved me over. "Good. You're here. This is a front-page story. You hear me?"

"Of course. But I'm not in charge of that. Klee decides, along with Silas."

Mabel grunted. "You own the paper, don't

you?" She looked me up and down. "What happened to you? Is this the new fashion?"

I looked down at my jeans, which were intact but stained with dirt. "I was communing with nature."

"Is that what's on your face? Nature? Never mind. Get in there. This is a big story. These tea party raves are going to transform this town. You know there's big business in senior living. Big! Where's your reporter's notebook? Don't you take notes? Maybe I should call Silas to do this story. Don't you people know a good story when you see it? Is that a worm crawling out of your ear?"

I slapped at my ear and took my notebook out of my purse and jotted down "senior living" and showed it to Mabel. She didn't look convinced about my competence.

She opened the door to the dining room. There were about fifteen large round tables set up, each with a white tablecloth and tea service on them. "Nobody else has this," Mabel bragged. "Nobody. Goodnight will bring in geezers by the hundreds to live here because of this. It'll revitalize the town. And they won't run scared into the wilds and have to be tracked down for two thousand a head. I can tell you that."

I wrote, "geezers" and "revitalize the town" in my notebook.

"Tea Party Rave. Is that what you're calling it?" I asked.

"Yes. The seniors here love it. They really party down. Work out a lot of energy. I had to expand the time because once they start partying, they don't want to stop."

"Cucumber sandwiches and Earl Grey tea?"

"And little cakes. Don't forget the little cakes."

I wrote "little cakes" in my notebook. The lights dimmed, and Frank Sinatra started crooning through the sound system. Seniors began filing into the dining room. Most walked, but about a third used walkers or wheelchairs. Sure enough, there was a general air of excitement.

"Come with me. I want to show you something," Mabel said. She took me to a control panel by the wall. "Don't forget to write about this. John Travolta would pee his pants to have this." She flipped several switches, and the room was transformed with swirling, colored lights and effects. Two people dropped to the ground in a dead faint. "Oh, damn. They forgot to take their anticonvulsants before they got here. Some of the patrons react badly to the special effects, but screw 'em. This here is Star Trek-level greatness. Don't write about the patrons and the convulsions."

"No problem."

The lighting effects changed again, and the two unconscious seniors came back to life, getting up from the floor and launching right into the Twist.

"What are you still doing here?" Mabel demanded. "Go and interview the happy seniors. Don't worry about photos. I emailed a bunch of them to Klee already."

I saluted her and walked to the nearest table. Two women were sitting, eating finger sandwiches, and a few others were swaying their hips nearby. "Take a sandwich. They're not bad," one of the women told me.

"Better than the slop they serve here, normally," the other said.

"How do you like the raves?" I asked.

"Great! Food and music. It sure beats bingo and petting those puppies they like to bring in to raise our happiness quotient."

"Happiness quotient," a man behind me sneered, and he spit on the ground.

One of the women leaned in close to me. "The lights horny the men up. The music moves the women, but the men get randy dandy from those lights."

The effects changed again, and a woman dropped to the floor.

"And I got a new room after old lady Phyllis dropped dead from the disco strobe," another woman told me. "An upgrade."

I wasn't sure what notes I should be taking. They were saying they loved the raves, but it sounded more like Abu Ghraib. I asked more questions, getting all the facts. The raves started after lunch in order to finish up before the early bird special. I hadn't eaten lunch, so I chowed down on the sandwiches, eating while I went from table to table. Most of the people were up dancing and flirting, especially when the music changed from Frank Sinatra to AC/DC.

"I don't dance," a woman told me, as I took a bite of one of the mini-cakes. "Bum hip. Bum knee. Bum other knee. And I don't have toes. You gotta have toes to really dance right. You know what I mean?"

She opened her purse on the table and dug through it, pulling out her belongings and placing them on the table next to it. Finally finding a Kleenex, she blew her nose loudly. In the middle of her belongings, I spotted a gold piece of paper. I recognized it immediately. It was a VIP Ticket to Heaven.

"What's that?" I asked her.

"That's my guarantee to get into heaven, that is. I'm going to sit at the right hand of God, and behind me will be a young guy named Paolo who will give me full body massages every day. *Full* body. You know what I mean?"

"Where did you get the ticket?"

"I paid a thousand dollars for it. I'm one of the lucky few. They're a limited issue, you know. There's not that many VIPs in heaven. There's me and Jesus and not too many more. Oh, and Paolo. He'll be there. That's guaranteed or my money back."

The hair on the back of my neck stood up. "Who did you buy it from?"

"A guy. I can't remember his name. Not bad looking."

My brain whirred into action, like all of my neurons were firing at the same time. I slapped the table hard and jumped up. "Margaret Marshall!" I yelled.

"I know Margaret," the woman said. "The meanest bitch in Goodnight. Although, she was always nice to me."

"Margaret Marshall! MM! The second set of initials." It was all tying in together. Leonard Shetland's letter was real. There were now three deaths, and I was sure they were connected. Somehow, I would have to save the person with the last set of initials.

PART II: A HOTTIE COOKS FOR MATILDA, AND ANOTHER HOTTIE COMES BACK TO TOWN

Falling Feces Stalk Townspeople
by Silas Miller

Nearly thirty people have reported that black goo has fallen from the sky, showering them in the substance. Local lab tests have revealed that the black goo is actually human poop.

"I don't know how, but someone up there is taking a dump, and it's landing all over our town," Goodnight Clinic lab technician Shemp Jones said.

Theories about the poop have abounded among locals. The most common theory is that the stool is coming from airplane toilets. "They're opening up those toilets and dumping it all over our town," local businessman Rocco Humphrey explained. "It's a cost-saving measure. That way, they don't have to clean up their own sh**. They just open the trap doors and whoosh! it falls on our heads."

But NTSB and FAA officials refute that claim. "Any plane over Goodnight, New Mexico, is flying at over thirty-thousand feet," John Thayer from the FAA said. "Even if the airlines could figure out a way to crap over America, the crap would diffuse out into the air. There wouldn't be any splat going on."

The poop incidents have happened all over town at different times of the day. Local officials have asked people to carry umbrellas and not to look up with their mouths open.

CHAPTER 5

I rushed home to write my story quickly and change my clothes in order to get to Amos's house in time. My brain swam with thoughts of the recent deaths, another dead girl talking to me, and the fact that Amos needed to ask me something.

What did he want to ask me? And did I need to shave my legs for it?

I flopped down at my desk and opened a new file for the Tea Party Raves' story. "What happened to your head?" Silas asked me.

"Is there another worm crawling out of my ear?" I asked, swatting at my ear.

"*Another* worm? How'd the rave go?"

"It ended early because one of the men had to go to the hospital. He forgot to take his medication before the rave. It was the first rave in history where someone was hospitalized for *not* taking drugs."

Silas laughed. "That's a good one, boss. Put that in the article. The readers will eat it up."

"I'm not sure Mabel will be happy about that."

"Who cares? We stir things up. We're watchdog journalism. W're the thin line between democracy and tyranny."

"So, I should put in the part about the seizures?"

I wrote the story in record time, and Silas ripped through it with his red pen and basically rewrote the whole thing. "You're doing much better, boss. You're going to be a great reporter."

Klee guffawed and said something under her breath that I couldn't make out. I told Silas about Margaret and the initials.

"I already wrote the story about Margaret," he said. "MM. That's right. You've got the nose, boss. Okay. We might have some kind of wacko, knocking off older folks. Keep on the story."

I was tempted to tell him about the dead girl and what she said, but again, I was worried about how he would react. And there was no way I was going to say anything in front of Klee. But the girl had given me a clue, and I needed to check up on it pronto. She said she shouldn't have run away.

"Silas, is there some way I can look up a list of runaways? Maybe missing children?"

"Sure. Is there something I should know?"

"Not yet."

I jotted down the information and left the office to get dressed. I would have to research the runaway angle when I got home, on my own time. I fed the dogs early and let them run wild in the forest for fifteen minutes. Then, I stood in front of my closet and tried to figure out what was proper attire to wear when a gorgeous man had something to ask.

I took out a long skirt and a sweater and went to the bathroom. "Oh my God!" I yelled when I finally saw myself in the mirror. My face looked like it had been dragged by wild horses. The tip of my nose was scabbed over, and there were twigs and dirt in my hair.

I looked like I had fallen off a cliff.

Quickly, I turned on the tap and dunked my head under it. I washed off as best as I could, but I still had skid marks on my cheek, and my nose looked like Rudolph the Flying Reindeer's. I put on a double-dose of makeup and slipped on the clothes as fast as I could. Whatever Amos had to ask me, I hoped he wouldn't be put off by my face.

Not that I cared about what he had to ask me. I was totally off men. And Amos was still in love with his wife. And there was Boone… who I didn't even like! But. Oh, who was I kidding? There was a hormonal soup bubbling up inside me, ready to boil over.

It was a beautiful drive to Amos's house. He lived south of town and had enough land to satisfy a militia in Montana. He was more or less J.R. Ewing, except he was way nicer and much better looking. His wife had decorated the inside of their house, and she did a beautiful job.

I crossed a bridge over the Snake River, and his ranch came into view. Horses were frolicking in a ring, and the house was already lit up inside. I parked in front, and Amos came out to greet me. He was out of his sheriff shirt and was wearing a tight white undershirt that showed off every bit of his torso. Holy cow, he was like a mutant of sexiness. I wondered if his mother had gotten bitten by some kind of radioactive spider when she was pregnant that made him look that good.

His brother Boone looked equally as good, although he was dusty and unkempt. Maybe their mother got bit by two radioactive spiders.

"You look a lot better than you did," he said. "I wasn't sure you were going to make it."

"I'm fine, and I wouldn't leave you in the lurch

when you have something important to ask me." My voice came out calm, like I wasn't dying of curiosity and half-hoping for a ring. Oh, geez. I was still married! Why was I hoping for a ring from Amos? We barely knew each other.

But he did have a giant ranch.

And a six-pack.

But what about his brother?

Well, Boone wasn't there. He had left without a word about where he was going.

But he had left me a nice note.

My brain needed a break. "Do you have a drink?"

"Gin and tonic?"

"That sounds good."

Inside, there was a crackling fire in the large fireplace, and candles lit up the great room. Holy cow. He was going to ask me something *big*.

He locked eyes with me. "I hope you're ready for something hot."

"Uh…" I said.

"Cause we're going to get hot right now."

He took my hand, and I followed him to his gourmet kitchen. The smell was out of this world delicious. My stomach growled. "Did you cook?" I asked. Amos was known for his cooking, and he had cooked for me once before. Then, dessert was his lips, and they were the highlight of the meal.

"I haven't stopped cooking for a week. It's too important now. This is going to be my year. Blue Ribbon," he said.

I had no idea what he was talking about. "Are you changing careers?"

"No, I'm a sheriff for life. The Chile Pepper Cook-off is this weekend. It's the event of the year in Goodnight. The Gazette does a huge thing for it. Haven't you guys been talking about the Chile Pepper Cook-off at the paper?"

"Maybe. I'm a day-to-day kind of reporter. They don't keep me in the loop much." Amos nodded, but I sensed he was judging me. I was the owner of the Gazette, but I was less in the loop than the fifteen-year-old paperboy.

He walked around the island and stirred a pan on the stove. "I've entered the Cook-off for the past thirty years, ever since I was old enough to hold a spoon. I've gotten the red ribbon every year. That's second place. That bastard Morris from the diner always beats me and grabs the blue ribbon. Not this year. I have a secret weapon. Two. And that's what I need to ask you. I need you to tell me which of my two secret weapons is the best to use against Morris."

"That's what you want to ask me?" I asked, sitting on a barstool. A wave of disappointment and relief hit me at the same time. Suddenly, I understood my feelings for Amos. I was attracted to him, but I didn't really want him.

So, I was either really stupid or really smart.

Amos dunked a wooden spoon into the first dish and raised it to my lips. "Green chiles *and* Hatch chiles *and* red chiles. A little spicy but not too much. Let me know if it's the best thing you've ever tasted."

It was the best thing I ever tasted and so was the second dish. I ate a full meal, tasting each dish, one after the other, but I couldn't decide which one he should enter in the Cook-off. With my belly full and the romance off the plate, I decided it was time to show Amos the letter from Leonard. I retrieved it from the bottom of my purse, and that's when I remembered that I had stolen a bunch of papers from his nightstand. Shimmering in the depths of my purse, I spotted a second VIP Ticket to Heaven along with Leonard's papers. Now I had two. One from Stella and one from Leonard. I gasped. It was a connection.

Handing the letter to Amos, I explained about the initials and that there was a T.E. somewhere out there who was in danger. Amos read the letter twice.

"I wonder if that's Tony Eddy," he said.

"Retired washer-dryer repairman."

I sucked in air. "There might be a crazy person killing old people in Goodnight."

"I'll give you a scoop on deep background."

"What's deep background?"

"Ask Silas. You ready? The labs just came back on Stella. She didn't have the flu. She was poisoned. And guess what? She was poisoned with vaginal soap."

"She drank vaginal soap?"

Amos blinked. "No, she used it down there. She was poisoned through her ying yang."

Both Amos and I were going to the meeting at the rec center about the giraffe problem. Mabel had supposedly called in two experts to handle it. I was going to cover the story with Silas, while Amos was going to stand by in case the meeting got out of hand.

Amos locked up the house, and I followed him back into town. When I got to the rec center, I pulled Silas aside.

"What's deep background?" I asked him.

"You can't use the information, but you can use it to find the information elsewhere. What'cha got, boss?"

I told him about the vaginal soap. "Death by

ying yang. That's a good headline, right?"

He patted my back. "You're learning. You know what else is interesting? Stella's stepson hated her. She was spending his inheritance. He complained about it all the time, since he was counting on that money for his retirement."

"Wait a minute. Isn't the deputy sheriff Adam Beatman Stella's stepson?"

Silas touched his nose and then pointed at me. "You catch on quick."

"Holy crap. What a story." I was practically drooling with anticipation at covering the story.

"Yeah, it's a shame we have to waste our time on giraffes when it looks like we have a crazed killer out there. Oh, well. Sometimes you have to do the boring stuff so that you can do the exciting stuff."

The rec center community room was crammed to the rafters. Every folding chair was occupied by a concerned townsperson, and there were plenty of people standing in the back and along the walls. At the front of the room, there were three chairs. Mabel was sitting on one of them. A petite, dainty lady about seventy years old, dressed in baggy khaki pants, a safari jacket, and a large brown hat sat next to her. The third chair vacant. Next to it, Rocco stood, awash in shame as if he was sent to stand in the corner in the school in *Little*

House on the Prairie.

I stood at the back of the room, but Silas motioned me to walk to the front. "Press!" he yelled at two unfortunates sitting there, and they got up for us, and we took their seats.

Mabel stood. "Quiet, everybody!" she yelled. "As you know, this giraffe thing has gotten way out of hand, and we're the laughingstock of the country."

"My cousin in Germany said we made it on the news there, too," a man called from the audience.

"I heard we were on the front page of the Papua New Guinea Daily News," a woman in the audience yelled.

Mabel shot Rocco the stink eye. "That's just great. We're international now. So, it's even worse than I thought. The good news is that I've brought in two experts to help us with this problem and get our town out of this mess and turn it around. My tea party raves are putting Goodnight on the map, but they can't do miracles when thirty giraffes were tossed out into the wilds of New Mexico. I mean, we hanged one of these creatures over a hundred years ago and to make up for it, we send giraffes out to freeze to death and get eaten by coyotes?" Her voice raised in pitch and volume, and she shot another stink eye at Rocco. "So finally, finally, finally, we're going to get this taken care of. We're going to gather those giraffes and send them to the place in Boise where they're treated like Madonna at the Red Door. Okay? Okay? And remember that my tea party raves take place every Tuesday and Saturday after lunch at the Goodnight Senior Center and will be expanded through the community as popularity grows. Tea party raves are fun, fun, fun! Now, let me introduce you to Fifi Swan. She's the director of the Giraffes are Love Society, and she's going to use her expertise to find these giraffes."

Fifi stood. "Giraffes are the noblest creatures," she said, sounding like she represented the Lollipop Guild.

"Speak up!" someone from the audience yelled.

"I fell in love with giraffes when I was a little girl," Fifi continued.

"Can't hear you!" a few yelled, but Fifi persisted, sounding like she had sucked helium.

"Giraffes are loyal and tender and sweet and so smart. If you ever commune with a giraffe, you are transformed. Like astronauts who see the Earth from space are transformed, giraffes change the way you look at the world. They uplift your soul."

"A giraffe ate my underpants when they were drying on the line in the backyard!" someone yelled. Fifi smiled and looked lost in her reverie about giraffes.

The door to the room flew open, and a large, grizzled man stomped in. He looked around with his eyes squinted into slits. He had a week's worth of growth on his face, and his lips were chapped and pursed tight. He was wearing gray pants, a gray shirt, and boat shoes. As he walked in, the entire room gasped and then there was generalized murmuring.

"Holy crap, Mabel brought in Quint," Silas whispered to me.

"Who's Quint?"

"Picture Stalin and Captain Ahab having a baby and then give him gnarly sun damage and a *really* bad attitude. That's Quint. I haven't seen him in years. I thought he got killed in a fight with a meter maid in Albuquerque when she shot him, but he seems fine."

Quint's knees cracked and creaked as he walked. He ran his fingernails down the wall behind Mabel and then stood in front of Fifi and pointed a gnarled finger at the audience. "I'll take care of your giraffe problem," he said in his gravelly voice. "For a price. You need an expert, and I'm the only one here who's taken on these demon creatures in the wild. You need an experienced hand at herding these vicious, sadistic, ruthless animals. And that's me."

Fifi stepped from behind him. "Actually, giraffes are gentle giants. Nature's sweetest gift to the world."

Quint growled at her. "Giraffes have lifeless eyes, black eyes, doll's eyes."

"Teddy bear eyes," Fifi said.

"Why do I think I've seen this before?" I asked Silas. "I've got a huge case of déjà vu."

"Giraffes are soulless, and you don't take notice of them until they're eating you," Quint growled.

"Actually, giraffes are herbivores," Fifi squeaked. Her happy, positive demeanor was waning, and it was getting replaced with a distinct amount of distress.

"I'll never go back to the savanna," Quint continued. "But I'll get these thirty for you safe and sound. I'll get their heads, tails, and everything in between, all alive and well and ready to be put in your zoo in Boise. But I want to be paid and paid well."

"Maybe we're on Candid Camera," I whispered to Silas.

"Is that show still on the air?" he asked me.

"No, seriously. This is a joke, right?" I asked Silas. "This doesn't seem familiar to you?"

"What're you talking about?"

"Does Steven Spielberg ring a bell?"

Mabel spoke up. "Rocco's offering two thousand a head, but no harm can come to them," she told Quint. Rocco held his head in shame.

"I'll do my best, but if they want war, I'll give

them war," Quint warned.

"Giraffes are noble and docile animals," Fifi pleaded.

Mabel looked at her watch. "The meeting is now over. I have to go home and work on the Chile Pepper Cook-off. There's a planning committee meeting tomorrow. I hope the giraffes will be taken care of by then," she added to Fifi and Quint.

"Mabel made a chaotic situation into a clusterfuck," Silas told me. "Bad for the town but not boring, right?"

Silas left to interview Fifi and Quint. I was in a hurry to get to my computer at the office to research the four victims and see what they had in common. I already knew two of them had bought VIP Tickets to Heaven. It was obviously a scam and the scammer was my number one suspect, but I didn't know why he would have killed them. I also wanted to search the runaway database to find the dead girl I spoke to at the bottom of the canyon.

Following the crowd, I made it to my car when Adele stopped me. She looked worn out. Her hair was messed, and she rubbed her eye. "I'm glad I caught you," she told me. "I tried to call Nora, but she's not answering. She's probably asleep already. I thought I should warn her."

"What's wrong?"

"It's about those witches she's working for. I heard that they cursed Leonard Shetland and then he dropped dead. And that's not all. I heard that for a few bucks, they'll curse anyone you want. Supposedly, their curses work. People have been dropping like flies."

CHAPTER 6

It was a busy Wednesday morning. Two more people got poop-bombed from the sky, and the potato burglar held up Goodnight Liquor. The manager shot at him, but missed, taking down three street lights in the Plaza, which put the all-important Chile Pepper Cook-off in danger of being canceled because the lack of light was a health hazard, even though the Cook-off was going to take place during the day.

So, Jack skipped school, again and helped Silas burn through the stories like they were the Avengers of local news. Meanwhile, I was burning up Google with searches on the witches and sifting through thousands of pictures of runaway girls.

I was getting nowhere fast, while Jack was typing seventy-words-per-minute with two fingers, writing the juicy details about the liquor store manager's brush with death by potato. I went outside for some fresh air, hoping to see Boone's truck, but he still hadn't come back from wherever he was.

"Fine. Then, I'm going to crowbar the shit out of his door and find out who this guy really is," I said out loud. As soon as the words came out of my mouth, I heard the sound of a vehicle drive toward the house. I sucked air and sucked in my stomach. I fluffed my hair and wondered if I had enough time to change my clothes.

But it wasn't Boone. It was Nora driving up in her Kia. I had called her last night, warning her not to get cursed. "I knew this job was too good to be true," she grumbled.

Now, she skidded to a halt behind Klee's Cadillac, turned off the motor and practically fell out of her car. "I told them I was going on errands," she breathed, wild-eyed and panicked.

"Come in. I'll give you milk," I said. I was pretty much out of everything else.

We walked into the house through the living room, and Nora almost fell into the hole in the floor. I grabbed her arm and pulled her out of harm's way just in time. "Are you digging to China?"

"Faye started a lot of work and then Jenny and

Joyce took her away from me."

"Oh my gosh. I forgot about Faye. What if they curse Faye?"

I had forgotten about Faye, too. But Faye was tough. "She has a hammer and a nail gun," I pointed out, and Nora nodded.

I gave her a glass of milk and a peanut butter sandwich. The dogs gave me guilt, so I made them a sandwich, too. We sat down at the kitchen table.

"I knew they were witchy and weird, but I didn't know about the curse. So, after we talked, I made some phone calls." Nora took a big breath and drank down some milk. "It turns out that Jenny and Joyce branched out from reading tea leaves and Tarot cards to curses about a month ago. Nobody will admit to hiring them, so I don't know who their clients are, but something bad is happening in that house, Matilda. Something *bad*."

Goosebumps sprouted on my arms. "They can't be real witches," I said, hoping Nora would confirm that.

"Of course not," she said, but we locked eyes and all kinds of unspoken words passed between us: I had spoken to two dead girls, so what kind of leap do you need to take to believe in curses?

"The initials were on that letter," Nora said after

a moment. "How did he know those people were going to drop dead?"

"Either they're really doing curses, it was a coincidence that the old people dropped dead, or Jenny and Joyce sealed the deal and bumped them off to make it seem like they could really do curses. You know, they could probably charge a fortune for curses once they prove they work. They could bring in money from all over the world for that."

"Oh, you're good, Matilda," Nora said, impressed. "You're like Jessica Fletcher."

I felt myself blush. "You think so?"

"Or Matlock. You could be Matlock, too."

"Wow, a lawyer. That would be something." I pictured myself in court in a nice suit for a moment, and then I remembered that Stella was murdered. "Vaginal soap."

"Excuse me?"

"Stella was poisoned with vaginal soap."

"She drank vaginal soap?"

"No, she was poisoned through her ying yang."

Nora crossed her legs. "That's possible? Killer ying yangs?"

"I guess so."

"Ying yangs cause a lot of problems, Matilda," Nora said. "My ying yang has a mind of its own."

I thought about that for a moment. "We need more information about Jenny and Joyce. We need to spy on them. I can't find information about them, and even with your network and Adele, the intelligence is slim. So, we need a man on the inside."

"You're right. Who should we get?" I stared at her, and she leaned back, as if she could escape my eyes. "No," she said, shaking her head.

"You're already there."

"No."

"You spend your days with them."

"No."

"You have access to their private records."

"No. No. No, Matilda. I don't want to be cursed. I don't want my ying yang to kill me. I don't like witches. No offense."

"None taken. I think. Look, they're probably not witches. They probably just murdered those old people to look like they're witches."

Nora stood and began to pace the kitchen floor. "That's your argument? They're only killers, not magical killers?"

"I didn't have a lot of time to think up a good argument. But Faye will be there. She's strong. She can bonk them with a hammer if they try to kill you."

"Faye! Faye can spy on them, and I'll go back to

the bank." Her face dropped, and she sat back down. "That stupid bank wasn't paying me enough. I really like this job, and it pays enough so that we can live. Do you know how expensive thirteen kids are?"

"I can't imagine. I'm on a peanut butter and jelly sandwich diet because I can't afford ham."

"Maybe they're innocent. Maybe they're nice ladies who've gotten a bad rap."

No way. There was something rotten in Witch Manor. "That's possible," I said.

"Okay. I'll do it. I'll be your rodent."

"You mean, mole."

"Isn't a mole a rodent?"

Nora left to spy on Jenny and Joyce, and I got the crowbar I kept next to my bed in order to break into Boone's place. Just as I had it positioned in his doorframe, Klee walked out of the Gazette office. She froze for a second when she saw me ready to do damage to Boone's door, but Klee was always put together and sophisticated, so she didn't bat an eye.

"Silas wants you. It's urgent," she told me.

I put the crowbar down on the ground and followed her back into the office. Silas was on the phone, talking animatedly. He waved me over to his desk.

"That's right. That's right. Okay. Fine," he said into the phone and hung up. "Boss, I need you to get a quote from Sheriff Goodnight."

"Okay," I said, picking up my phone. Silas took the receiver from me and slammed it down.

"No. Listen. You need to get a quote from Amos. But he's not reachable by phone. Otherwise, I would have called him. He's out fly fishing up where Snake River meets Yellow River. You got that?"

I had no idea where Snake River met Yellow River. I had never heard of Yellow River. "Yes. Got it."

"Good. Listen, carefully. Deputy Sheriff Adam Beatman was arrested and charged with the murder of his stepmother, Stella Hernandez."

I gasped and stumbled backward. "What? But what about the witches?"

"Forget about them. Adam Beatman gave his stepmother vaginal soap for her birthday."

Who gives their stepmother vaginal soap for her birthday, poisoned or not? It sounded like Adam should get jailed just for giving creepy birthday presents. "Poisonous vaginal soap," I said.

Silas's face brightened, which was saying something because he already had a euphoric glow to him, faced with a big scoop. "Deep background, right, boss? I like your moxie. Jack and I are running the story over here, but we need a quote from the sheriff. You got me? We can't run this without a quote directly from him. That's on you. You have to track him down and make him talk, write down what he says and bring it here or better yet, call it in to me."

"There's no cell service over there, remember," Klee reminded him.

"That's right," Silas said, remembering. "So go over there and get that damned quote and run it back to me. Boss, run it back to me. It's more important than Christmas. You get what I'm saying? You wouldn't want to go without Christmas, would you?"

I shook my head no. "I like Christmas."

"Then go. Here. Jack marked it on a map. No GPS out there, either. Go! The free world depends on you!"

"Holy crap!" I exclaimed, grabbed the map and my purse, and ran out of the office.

It turned out that I was no good at reading maps. Who the hell uses maps anymore? I never had, and it didn't look like now was the time for me to start. I drove for an hour, got lost in the wilderness, and was sure I was going to get eaten by a bear. But finally,

finally like Moses finally finding the Promised Land, I spotted Amos's SUV by the bank of the roaring river. I couldn't park next to him because my Altima was not a four-wheel drive. So, I parked up the hill on the dirt road, nestled between trees and climbed down the hill through the trees to get to the river.

"Hello!" I called over the roar of the water. It was a hell of a place to go fishing. Beautiful, but in the middle of nowhere and so wild that it was scary. "Amos! It's me, Matilda!"

Nothing. No sign of him. I peeked through the driver's window of his car, and he wasn't in there, either. He had to be out there somewhere, but I didn't know where. At the shore of the river, I looked to my left and to my right. Would he go upstream or downstream to fish? What did salmon do? Were there salmon in New Mexico?

Downstream was a straight line from his car. I could see far down the shore, which was comforting, but I could see that he wasn't that way. So, I decided to go upstream, around the corner where the river turned and I would probably get lost and eaten by a bear.

"Hello!" I called. "Amos, it's Matilda!"

I heard movement in the bush next to me, and I broke out into a run. A few minutes into my run, I saw him. Amos was standing waist deep in the river. He was wearing waders, which came up to his torso, and he wasn't wearing a shirt. The water rushed by his body as he lifted one muscular arm up and flicked the line of his fishing rod back and forth over his head, teasing the water.

"Hello, there!" I shouted. Amos turned in surprise and almost slipped, but caught his balance, quickly. "I need a quote!" I yelled over the sounds of the river.

"A coat?" he called back.

"A quote. A quote."

I stepped forward, but he gestured for me to stop. He walked out of the river and stood on the shore. "What's up? Did Goodnight burn down?"

"I need a quote about Adam Beatman's arrest," I said, taking my reporter's notebook out of my purse. His chest was very distracting, and my eyes kept flicking to it.

"No comment."

"Just a little one?"

"No comment."

His face was set in stone. Impassible. There was no way he was going to tell me anything.

"Pleasssse," I whined. "Silas is going to kill me if I don't get something. This is a big story, you know. Deputy Sheriff kills woman with vaginal soap."

Amos looked down at me and blew out, as if he decided that he didn't have a choice. "He was arrested on *suspicion*. Nothing is decided yet. All right. I'll give you my statement. Are you ready? Your pen is clicked on?"

I clicked my pen. "Ready."

"The Goodnight Sheriff's Department doesn't comment on ongoing investigations."

He stared me down, but there was a hint of a smile on his lips. "Really? Is that a real thing? Nothing? You can't give me anything? Why did Adam Beatman buy his stepmother vaginal soap? That's a weird gift."

Amos shrugged. "I don't know. He says a woman at the store suggested it as a gift. Deputy Beatman is suspended with pay pending the investigation. That's about all I can give you. Do you have anything to add?"

"Me?" I asked.

"You. Trouble. You. The snoop hound Matilda Dare. You must have found out a lot of things. What can you tell me?"

I could tell him that I had been wrong. I had thought the murders were all related. I never saw the Adam thing coming. I could have told Amos about the witches and the curses, too. That was probably illegal. But I didn't know anything for sure, and Silas would skin me alive if I divulged my story before it was written.

"Matilda Dare doesn't comment on an ongoing investigation," I said, finally.

"That's what I figured. How about my entries for the Cook-off? Have you thought about it?"

"They were both delicious," I said, honestly, and my stomach growled. "They're both winners."

"Or both second-prizers." He sighed. "I can't decide which one to enter. That's why I'm out here. Trying to clear my head with fly fishing. You want to try?"

"I'm not a good swimmer." And I had had an unfortunate experience a couple weeks ago when a large man fell on me in a swimming pool.

"You stand. You don't swim. Never mind. I forgot you're Trouble."

He punched me playfully on the shoulder. Ah, the playful, pal shoulder punch. Whatever romance that had been between us was dead and buried. The gorgeous, rich cowboy sheriff was happy to look at pictures of his dead wife, cook, and go fly fishing. Not that I cared, I reminded myself. I was totally off men.

Amos walked back into the water with his fishing rod, and I ran back toward my car to bring the pathetic non-statement to Silas. I walked around the bend and almost made it to Amos's SUV when I noticed someone on the other side of the river. I squinted, trying to make out the figure. It was a short person, thin…

Oh my God.

I ran down the embankment and stood right where the water touched the shore to get a better view. It was the dead girl from the bottom of the canyon. She was wearing the same outfit, and she pointed at me and said something.

"What?" I called. She said something, again. I took a couple of steps into the river, but I still couldn't hear her. I waded deeper in until the water went up to my thighs.

"What?" I called again.

She pointed at me. "He's closer than you think," she said.

CHAPTER 7

"He is?" I asked and took one more step toward her. One step too many.

The water knocked me off balance, and I sailed away downstream. I kicked my legs and dog-paddled my arms, but the river was taking me, and I was powerless to right myself.

"Help!" I yelled and got a mouthful of river that went down the wrong pipe and made me choke, violently. I clutched my purse to my chest and started spinning. First, I was like a corkscrew and then I started doing somersaults. My whole life I wasn't flexible, and I never could get through a gymnastics class, but now I was Gabby Douglas.

And it was going to kill me.

"Hel…" I yelled and got another gallon of water

down my gullet.

This was it. This was the end. Still married to a murderer, a pathetic fledgling reporter, and a sort of homeowner with a large hole in her living room floor. That was the grand sum of my life. What would Jack write for my obituary? *She never did anything, but she smelled good. And she was crazy. And she spoke to dead people.*

Oh, no. That was a terrible obituary.

I needed to live longer so I could have a better obituary!

Round and round I went underwater. My shoes flew off, and rocks scraped my feet. I tried to scramble to the top and get air, but the current was too strong for me. I was completely out of control and doomed to be killed by the raging river.

Funny how when you think all is lost and you give up hope, someone or something decides otherwise for you. That's what happened with me. Just as I was going down for the last time, a strong hand grabbed me and pulled me out of the water.

I gulped air. "I'm drowning," I moaned.

"No, you're not. I got you." He was large, strong, and muscular. He was behind me, his arm around my chest, pulling me in tight against him so my head would stay above water. The dead girl's voice came back to me. *He's closer than you think.*

"Help! Killer! Help!" I shouted and fought against the man. I managed to extricate myself from his grasp with a sharp elbow to his face. But then I was helpless again, carried away by the current, and so was the man this time. The current was stronger now, and we were picking up speed.

"Sonofabitch," the man growled with his back to me.

The "sonofabitch" sounded familiar. "Boone?" I asked. "Is that you?" He turned around. "What're you doing here?"

"Saving you," he spat. "Why did you elbow me in the face?"

"I thought you were a serial killer who kept young girls locked up in a dungeon somewhere."

"Great judge of character. How did you know about the dungeon?"

The water pulled me down, and he managed to pull me back up, but he was having trouble too against the current. I grabbed on to him, wrapping my arms around his neck and my legs around his waist.

"Your purse is hitting the back of my head," he complained. "You're pulling me down. For the love of God, kick your feet." I kicked my feet. "Not my balls! Not my balls! Kick in the other direction. Oh, never mind. We're going to make it to that tree at the side."

"The log over there? We'll never make it. It's too far. The current's too strong."

"Then we're going to die because the Yellow River is about to spill into the Snake River, and it does it with level five rapids."

"That sounds bad," I said.

"We got to get to the tree now. Kick! Kick! Kick! We got to do it now!"

With the sound of the rapids getting louder, I kicked with everything I had. Boone did most of the work, though, and miraculously, we made it to the log. We held on tight to it. Boone was wet and sexier than I remembered. Wherever he had been during the past two weeks, he had gotten weatherworn. His hair was longer, but his face was clean shaven and tan. I caught him studying me, too, and I could only imagine how I looked.

"We'll be fine now," Boone said. "As soon as we catch our breaths, we'll make it the rest of the way to the embankment."

This part of the river had steep, muddy embankments on either side, and it would be difficult to climb out of the river. "Okay," I said.

"What were you doing in the river?" he asked.

I was talking to a dead girl. "I fell in."

"You fell into the river out in the middle of nowhere?"

"I was interviewing Amos and then I was going to my car, and I fell in."

"You were interviewing Amos? Is that what the young people are calling it these days?"

He was jealous, and I loved that he was jealous. "I don't like your tone, Boone. I don't like what you're insinuating, and I'm insulted. I'm a professional journalist. I needed to get an important statement about Adam Beatman's arrest."

"What're you talking about?"

"Adam Beatman was arrested for poisoning his stepmother's vaginal soap."

Boone blinked. "How much river water did you drink?"

I ignored his question. "All kinds of people have died since you left." I told him about Leonard's letter, the witches, and the dead old people.

"Margaret Marshall is the meanest bitch in Goodnight, but she's always been nice to me."

"Was. She fell off a cliff. I fell on top of her. Well, not on top. Near her."

"Before you came to town, the most exciting thing that ever happened in Goodnight was the annual two-for-one toothpaste sale at Goodnight Pharmacy. It's like you opened the portal to hell or something."

"Amos calls me 'trouble.'"

Boone scowled at me. "He did, did he? You've been talking a lot to Amos."

I shrugged, which was hard because the water was cold, and I was shivering pretty intensely. "He cooked for me."

"Ah, the Chile Pepper Cook-off. It's his lifelong goal to get the blue ribbon."

"Do you cook?" I asked him.

"I toasted a Pop-Tart once, but I burned it. C'mon, we better get you out of this water, or you're going to get hypothermia."

"I'm ready," I said and let go of the log. "Oh no! My purse!" My purse was carried off by the river, and I grabbed for it.

"Don't! It's just a purse!" Boone called.

"My wallet and car keys are in it. And my reporter notes."

And then it was too late. My swimming turned into uncontrolled floating. I was swept away toward my purse.

"Sonofabitch," I heard Boone complain. "You're determined to kill me."

"I got my purse!" I called, managing to grab it, but I was being pulled away fast.

"Swell!" he yelled back and kicked off from his safety at the log.

It didn't take long for him to catch up to me and grab hold of my arm. The water was moving at a violent speed and bringing us along with it at a fast clip. I looked back longingly at our log. There was no way to get back to it. We were powerless against the current.

"Keep your knees up," Boone ordered. "It might help protect you from breaking your neck."

"I don't want to break my neck."

"Then keep your knees up."

"I can hear the rapids."

"You know why you can hear the rapids?" he asked, not too patiently. "Because we're about to die in them." Boone took one of my hands, and I held onto my purse with my other hand. "Don't forget, Matilda. Knees up."

It was bad, nothing like a ride at Disneyland. The water threw me around like a rag doll, and the only thing that kept me up was Boone. Twice, he tugged me out of the way of a large rock. I gulped water, which made me cough and sputter.

"It's going to get bad, now," Boone warned over the sound of the rapids.

"It's *going* to get bad? It's not bad, already?"

"But it's okay because you have your purse. It

would be really bad if you didn't have your purse."

"I don't like your tone," I said, just as he pulled me out of the way of a boulder.

"This is it, Matilda. Fill your lungs with air."

He gripped my hand hard and then it all went to hell. I was completely at the mercy of the water. Nature is a cruel bitch. Probably a lot meaner than Margaret Marshall. It took us about two minutes to get through the rapids, but it felt like an hour. But we made it through.

"We made it! We're alive," I said, euphoric. On the other side of the rapids, the water was smooth as glass, but the current was still strong. "That wasn't too bad."

"Swim to the side. Come on. The falls are coming."

"What falls?"

He swam full out for the side of the river, but he was still holding onto my hand, and I was holding him back, no matter how much I tried to keep up. I wanted to tell him to save himself and swim to safety on his own, but I was a coward and didn't want to break my neck or drown by myself. So, I kept swimming even though my strength was leaving me, and I threatened Boone's life with my added weight. It didn't seem like we were making much progress. It was like a nightmare where I had no strength and couldn't move as much as I tried. I was so tired, and the water was so cold.

Then, all went black.

I woke up lying with my face in the mud, and Boone peeling my cold, wet clothes off my body. "What happened?" I croaked.

"Well, you tried really hard to kill me, but I survived."

"Did we go down the falls?"

"No, for some wacky reason you swam in the wrong direction toward the falls, but I knocked you out, flipped you on my back and swam you back to shore against impossible odds and a breakneck current. I saved your life. You're alive because of me. Now I'm taking off your clothes so you don't catch pneumonia."

I rolled over and wiped some mud off my face. "You knocked me out?"

"You might have a bruise on your jaw. I hear arnica's good for that."

I sat up. "I'm not wearing pants. You're not wearing pants."

"Hell of a first date. Am I right?" he asked, and his eyes flashed big and dark. "I only had to get you in a near-death experience to get your pants off."

"My purse!"

Boone picked it up from the ground, making a sucking sound as it was pulled out of the mud. "Your purse is intact. I've never met a woman so attached to her purse."

"It's leather." Boone tugged at my shirt. "What're you doing? I'm cold. I don't want to be naked."

Normally I would have wanted to be naked with Boone, if I were completely honest with myself. But I was shivering something awful, and my hands and feet hurt from the cold so much that I didn't feel a thing on my jaw where Boone had knocked me out.

"I know it's counter-intuitive, but first we need to get your clothes off and then I'll start a fire. When you get half-defrosted, we'll walk back to my truck, and I'll crank up the heat."

It was a plan. And since I didn't have one of my own, I decided to let Boone have one for me. He pulled my shirt off me and tossed it in the mud. I was down to my bra and panties, and Boone was only wearing black boxer-briefs. "I'll be right back," he said, sticking a finger up in the air.

Then, he was gone. I was sitting in the cold mud, and the wind was blowing. I figured that there was a seventy percent chance that Boone had abandoned me, and I was going to die alone in the middle of the wilderness. But dying of cold wasn't as glamorous as it sounded, and after five minutes of waiting for Boone, I was praying that a bear would come and eat me fast to put me out of my misery.

"Here I am," Boone said, arriving with his arms piled high with wood. He dropped them on the ground and quickly arranged them in a pyramid. Then, he rubbed two sticks together, and presto chango, there was a large fire. I scooted closer to it. Boone sat down next to me and put his arm around me.

"You'll warm up in a minute," he said.

"You did that like a Boy Scout."

"Goodnight men learn how to make a fire before they learn to walk."

"What else do they learn to do?" I asked, and I could feel him tense. A rush of warmth went through my body, and it had nothing to do with the fire.

"Do you want a list?" he asked.

I gnawed on the inside of my cheek. "How was your trip?" I asked, deciding on a safer topic of conversation.

"Fine. Uneventful."

He was Mr. Mysterious, and that made all my warning lights flash. My husband had a lot of secrets that I wasn't aware of…like trying to put me away so he could get an inheritance.

Boone picked up his wet shirt and wiped at my face. "You had snot all over your cheek," he explained.

"Oh."

"Don't worry. I've seen worse."

"Gee. Thanks."

The fire was big and crackled loudly. The heat felt wonderful. Finally, I stopped shivering.

"Margaret Marshall fell off a cliff? She was way too mean to fall off a cliff," Boone said.

"What do you mean?"

"Just that it's more likely that someone pushed that bitch."

My ears pricked up. "Do you know who?"

"Well, her meanness was focused on one target in particular, but he's the nicest person in the world. Still, it's possible that he cracked finally."

"Who?"

"Her oldest son. Bernard."

Wow. It was a free-for-all against mothers. "What about Adam Beatman? Do you think he could have killed his stepmother?"

Boone rubbed his chin. "Oh, yeah. Adam was counting down to his retirement, and his father was going to fund it until he met that woman. Getting her out of the way was fundamental for him, so killing her would have been a no-brainer for Adam. But poisoned vaginal soap? Nuh-uh. Adam wouldn't have gone near that."

"It was proven that he bought her vaginal soap as a present," I pointed out.

"There must be a story there. But no way did Adam poison her. Listen, Adam Beatman has hunted every piece of meat that has ever gone in his mouth. He can kill an animal with any kind of firearm, knife, or snare. He's a hands-on kind of killer. He's not going to poison a woman's vagina."

I wasn't so sure his argument was valid. Maybe it was easier to kill a deer than it was to kill his father's wife. Maybe poisoning was a gentler way to go in Adam's mind and that's why he did it.

There were so many dead people and so many suspects. One thing was certain, I needed to look deeper into each of the deaths and get to the truth before the killer or killers struck again.

CHAPTER 8

Once we were warmed up, Boone doused the fire, and we walked to his truck, which was parked deep in the woods. He wet a dirty towel and handed it to me to clean myself as best as I could. Then, he tossed me a pair of sweatpants and a t-shirt to wear.

"Turn around," I told him.

"I've already seen your bra and panties. I'm seeing them right now." He scanned my body, and I squirmed under his gaze.

"I'm going to take them off. They're wet, and wet panties can give me an infection."

"Like strep throat?"

"Like a yeast infection. Like fungus." Boone frowned, looked up at the sky, and sighed loudly. "What's wrong?" I asked.

"Nothing. I was hoping that that would turn me off, but I'm still attracted to you."

My body reacted, and I got a big dose of cotton mouth. "Turn around," I croaked.

He turned, and I quickly peeled off my bra and panties. "Giraffes are gentle giants, not monsters that have to be defeated," I heard a woman plead. It was Fifi Swan. I would have recognized her squeaky, helium voice anywhere. She came into view, following Quint, who pulled a yellow barrel behind him with a thick rope. In a panic, I jumped into the sweatpants and held the t-shirt against my chest.

"Have you seen any giraffes?" Fifi asked us.

"Run for your lives, townspeople," Quint growled. "There be man-eating giraffes out here. Lifeless eyes. Doll's eyes."

"They're beautiful beings!" Fifi whined, running after him into the forest.

I put the t-shirt on and got in the truck. Boone got dressed too and slipped behind the steering wheel. "Do I want to know what that was about?" he asked me.

"Probably not."

"That looked like the guy from *Jaws*."

"Thank you! I thought I was the only one who noticed that."

Boone looked me up and down. "Yep. You

opened the portal to hell."

"Look, we really don't have a lot of time to sit here and insult me. We have to interview the mean bitch's abused son."

"We?"

Even with all of my focus on saving my purse, I had lost my keys and my cell phone. They had fallen out somewhere and were probably at the bottom of the falls. So, we left my car in the woods. Boone drove, and soon we were on a road toward town. Wiping myself down with a wet towel hadn't done a great job of removing all of the mud and sand. There was a bunch wedged in where I couldn't get at it, and it was making a lot of friction in a bad way. I tried to adjust myself in my seat, but it was no use. Boy, was I going to have a rash. On the way to Margaret's, I called Silas with Boone's phone, which he had kept in his truck. Silas wasn't thrilled with the quote, but he wasn't surprised.

Margaret lived high in the mountains, but her house was nothing like Jenny and Joyce's. Where they lived in a mansion, her house was small and squat; one story that looked like it was built in the late sixties and was never updated.

Boone parked in the driveway, next to an old

Toyota Celica. "Don't let the house fool you," he told me. "It may look modest, but it's attached to about thirty acres. Margaret was richer than Midas."

"That's more reason for Bernard to have killed her," I said.

"Yes, but wait until you meet him."

Bernard opened the front door of the house. He was average height and doughy. His clothes were worn but clean, and he didn't make eye contact. His hand flew to his face when he spoke, like he was trying to hide. "Hey there, Boone. My mom fell and died."

"I heard, Bernard. I'm so sorry. That's why I'm here, to say I'm sorry."

"You have mud on your face."

"We fell in the river."

"Why'd you do that?"

The conversation kept drifting. I could tell that Boone was trying to center Bernard, but it was difficult. Boone maneuvered us into the house, and Bernard invited us to sit on the couch in the living room. "How about you? You want to sit?" Boone asked Bernard as he hovered over us.

"Mother says I'm not allowed to sit on the furniture. My butt makes marks on it. Except the one chair in the kitchen. I'm allowed to sit on that."

Boone flashed me a look, which said "I told you

so. Meanest bitch in Goodnight."

"You want to bring the chair here so you can sit?" I asked Bernard. "Or we could all sit in the kitchen?"

Bernard's face brightened but then fell. "I'm not sure mother would like that. Remember the time in eighth grade, Boone?"

"Bernard went on a field trip to Santa Fe with us," Boone explained to me. "And his mother came down on him hard because he was a worthless lowlife that didn't deserve to go anywhere."

"She said that?" I asked.

"No, I was toning it down," Boone said. "She actually said he was a piece of shit that would never amount to anything, just like his father and then what did she do to you, Bernard? Lock you in the closet?"

"She has a box under her bed. She put me in that."

"Excuse me?" I asked.

"Like a coffin," Boone told me and arched an eyebrow.

"She put you in a coffin?" I asked. Margaret was the meanest bitch in Goodnight. I was so happy she was dead. I wish I would have pushed her off the cliff myself. Poor Bernard. I needed a drink. "You don't have anything to drink, do you?"

"Like iced tea?" Bernard asked.

"Okay."

"No, we don't have any iced tea."

"Oh," I said. "How about some chips?"

"No, Mother didn't let me snack."

"Even a peanut?" I asked. He shook his head. "Not one nut? Not a celery stalk with peanut butter? Not a cracker? Not even a saltine?" I asked.

"You can have half of my ham sandwich, if you don't mind partially stale bread," Bernard offered. "You want to see where Mother fell?"

"Not really," Boone said at the same time I said, "Yes, that's a good idea."

I passed on the ham sandwich, and we followed Bernard out back. The view was spectacular, but not quite as spectacular as the one from Jenny and Joyce's mansion. There was no fence in the back, but there was a small ridge that acted as a barrier and protection from falling. I couldn't see how a woman who lived here since the beginning of time would all of a sudden plunge to her death from her backyard.

"Nice view," Boone said.

"The one where she fell is better," Bernard said, as we followed him along the ridge past the house. "She fell at my special, private place."

I caught Boone's eyes, and he shrugged.

"Here we go," Bernard said five minutes later. We had reached a precarious spot on top of the canyon. A perch so high up that it made me nervous, and I took a few steps back until I was standing behind Boone. "It was right here," Bernard said, taking a couple steps to his left. He turned around so that his back was to the precipice, and his feet were balanced on a thin line of dirt that separated him from life and death. He was totally unconcerned about the height.

"She just fell right down, and then she was dead," Bernard continued. "They told me that all her bones were broken except for her toes. Her toes must have been stronger than usual. I think my toes are strong, too," he said, looking at his shoes.

"Did you see her fall?" I asked.

Bernard shook his head and continued to look at his shoes. "I wasn't here."

"But this is your special, secret place?" Boone asked. "Was it your mother's special, secret place, too?"

Bernard's face shot up, and his expression was all about the lightning bolt, ah-ha moment. "No. She never came up here. Why was she here?"

It was a good question.

Boone and I argued the entire way to Jenny and

Joyce's. He wanted to go home, and I wanted to spy on the witches and find out if they were murderers.

"I just need ten minutes at home," he said.

"This is on the way to home. It's in this neighborhood. Why are you making this such a big deal?"

"My balls, okay?"

"Is that code?"

"My balls. My balls," he said, his voice rising.

"What are you? LeBron James?"

Boone's jaw clenched. "Not basketballs. My balls are sandy. The friction is horrible."

"Oh, please. Your balls have nothing on my vagina. It's like I'm carrying a pocketful of dirt between my legs."

The truck swerved, but Boone righted it, quickly. "You're not a typical kind of woman, Matilda."

"I know, but I keep trying. Listen, the sisters must have a dozen bathrooms. I'm sure you could wash your balls in one of them."

"Perfect," Boone grumbled. "Nice to meet you, I'm Boone Goodnight. May I wash my balls in your bathroom?"

"Exactly," I said. "A very simple solution."

When we arrived, Boone parked behind Nora's car. He checked something in the back of his truck, which he was careful not to let me see, and then I went to the front door and rang the doorbell. It took a minute, but Nora answered the door in a full panic.

"You're here," she said in a loud whisper. "Thank goodness."

Faye appeared behind her with her hammer held high. "Is it a killer? Someone cursed?" She was whispering loudly, too.

"It's me," I whispered loudly back to them.

Faye lowered her hammer. "Come in," Nora urged, taking my hand. Boone and I followed her into a small side room. Faye closed the door with a soft click.

"I'm so glad you're here," Nora said, quietly and then stopped when she seemed to notice Boone for the first time. "Boone Goodnight. What're you doing here?" she asked while looking at me.

"I have sandy balls," he said and shrugged.

"I'm so confused," Faye said. "Did you get the wrong brother, Matilda? What happened with the question?"

"What question?" Boone asked, suspiciously.

"Nothing," I said. "The question wasn't an important question. And then I fell in the river, so that's why Boone's here."

Nora and Faye nodded slowly. "Are those your clothes?" Nora asked me.

"No, they're Boone's clothes," I said.

"She didn't want fungus in her vagina," Boone explained and smirked.

Nora nodded slowly, again. "I see. Are you wearing his underpants, too?"

"No. I'm not wearing any underpants. But it's not what you think," I added when I caught their shocked expressions.

"She has a pocketful of dirt between her legs," Boone explained.

I turned toward him. "Look, stop talking about my crotch."

"You started it. You talked about your crotch first."

"Yes, but I don't want you spreading it around."

"Understood," he said and smirked, again. "Don't spread your crotch around."

"I'm so confused," Faye complained. "What's going on?"

"It doesn't matter," Nora said. "We have more important stuff to talk about, and we have to be quick. Jenny and Joyce are doing a reading, and they'll be done in about fifteen minutes."

Nora took my hand again, and we went upstairs to a large bathroom. Nora pulled the shower curtain aside and grabbed a plastic bottle off the lip of the tub.

"Look," she said, handing me the bottle.

"Vaginal soap," I breathed.

"The same one that Stella used," Faye said.

My brain worked overtime and came up with a half-dozen nefarious theories about Jenny and Joyce.

"That's not all," Nora said. She put the vaginal soap back and ran us downstairs to her opulent office. She sat down at her computer and opened a drawer, pulling out some paper. "Look at this. They actually wanted me to put it in a file on the computer."

It was a list of names. *Stella Hernandez. Tony Eddy.* And further down on the paper: *Margaret Marshall.* At the very top of the paper was written *Cursed.*

"You see?" Nora whispered. "Witches."

"Look at that, sister. Our atomic karma sister has returned." It was Jenny with Joyce. They walked in, making the four of us jump in surprise. Faye lifted her hammer high, and Nora slapped the paper down on the desk.

"Who's this?" Joyce asked, taking Boone's hand in hers. She closed her eyes, and Jenny's eyes rolled back in her head.

"Boone Goodnight, ma'am," Boone said. For the first time, I saw his resemblance to Amos, beyond just physical characteristics. Western, gentlemanly charm oozed from his pores, just like his brother. "Nice to meet you."

Joyce's hands moved up his muscular arm until she was caressing his shoulder and his chest. "I'm sensing nakedness coming from you, Mr. Goodnight."

"I was hoping for a shower," he said, smiling.

"You can use mine," Jenny offered, excitedly.

"No, you'll use mine," Joyce said, firmly.

"Mine is bigger. He's big, sister. So big."

Jenny and Joyce were a few seconds away from drooling. It was the perfect time to both distract them and interrogate them at the same time. "I see dead people!" I shouted and walked out of the room like a zombie. The sisters followed me down the hall. When I turned into a room, I rounded on them. "I hear you can curse people," I whispered.

They leaned forward. "Oh, yes. Do you need someone cursed? Like Klee? We've been waiting for someone to ask to curse her," Jenny said, hopefully.

Joyce nodded in agreement. "She's a real bitch."

"Have you cursed a lot of people?" I asked.

The sisters exchanged a look. "We can't say," Joyce said. "Professional rules, you know."

Drat. "Have you had a lot of clients asking you to curse people?" I asked.

"They're not clients," Jenny insisted. "They're

souls in need."

"And there's souls in need confidentiality rules. So we can't tell you," Joyce said. "Are there dead people here now that you can see?"

"No," I said. "Once a day is enough for me. Have you seen any dead people lately? Any girls asking for help?"

Jenny pointed at me. "The murdered girl. You talked to her. We heard about that. What did she say?"

I sighed. I was hoping they were on the up and up and could give me more insight into the dead girls I had been talking to, but they were totally in the dark, and I had the sneaking suspicion they were gray-haired con artists who wore a lot of rings. The question was, were they murderer con artists?

"Are you getting paid by the sheriff to talk to the dead girls?" Joyce asked me. They leaned in, waiting for my answer.

"No."

"Stupid," Jenny said. "You could probably work out a monthly retainer that'll pay your bills."

Yep. They were con artists.

"Leonard Shetland, Margaret Marshall, Stella Hernandez, Tony Eddy," I said. "What did you do to them? I know you cursed them."

"No, we didn't," Jenny said.

Joyce shushed her.

I put my hands on my hips and gave them my best scowl. "I *know* you cursed them."

"You better be quiet or we'll curse *you*," Joyce warned.

"So you did curse them," I said, proud of myself.

"We didn't," Jenny said. "We were going to, but then something happened, and we couldn't do it."

"What happened?" I asked.

"We were interrupted," Joyce said. "And that's all we're going to say."

"What do you mean you were interrupted? Who interrupted you?"

"Sorry to interrupt you, but I really need to get home," Boone said, walking into the room. I shot him a death stare.

"You're not interrupting," Joyce gushed at him, and Jenny nodded in agreement.

"You're interrupting," I growled. "You're interrupting a lot. Go away and come back later when you're not interrupting."

"I need to get home, Matilda. I *need* to get home," Boone said.

I stomped my foot. "You haven't been home for weeks, and now all of a sudden you have to go home?"

He put his hand on my back and pushed me out of the room. "Look, something is crawling in my pants. Something I don't want crawling in my pants. I want to go home, strip down, and scrub myself down. Got it?"

"You can do that here," I said.

"With the poisonous vaginal soap? I don't think so."

He picked me up and marched me through the front door. Faye and Nora ran out after us. Boone opened the passenger door of his truck and tossed me in. "Should we keep spying?" Nora asked me through the open window.

"They're still suspects," I told them, as Boone started the engine. "But be careful. They might be dangerous."

"I've got Nora covered," Faye announced, punctuating each word with her hammer, like she was conducting a symphony for HGTV.

PART III: MATILDA FINDS ANOTHER VICTIM, AND BOONE DRESSES UP

Cheating Couple Found Asphyxiated in Car, Chile Pepper
Cook-off Threatened
by Jack Remington

Late last night, George Henry and Lisa Alcott were discovered dead in the latter's car. The couple is believed to have died from carbon monoxide, due to the running car in the closed garage.

"The deaths appear to be accidental," Patrolman Wendy Ackerman explained. "The couple was found naked and let's say, connected."

It's unclear why Henry and Alcott kept the car on, except maybe to keep the radio playing while they were together in the car. According to sources, the radio was tuned to the Arizona Diamondbacks game.

"If you didn't think the bastard was dumb before, you sure do now," Mr. Henry's wife, Julie Henry said. "And why would he have an affair with Lisa Alcott? The woman wasn't exactly Farrah Fawcett, you know."

Henry and Alcott were the organization and publicity chairs for the Goodnight Chile Pepper Cook-off, and their tragic and untimely deaths have threatened the event.

According to Mabel Kessler, the president of the Cook-off, the two left many details of the event's organization unknown and disappeared with them.

"It's a complete disaster," Kessler said. "We don't know which way is up. The posters? We don't know where they are. And where the hell are the chafing dishes?"

The mayor has called an emergency meeting to discuss the future of Saturday's Cook-off. "Giraffes, poop from the sky, a crazy potato burglar, and now no Chile Pepper Cook-off? Is this Goodnight, New Mexico or Florida?" the mayor asked.

The question is yet to be answered.

CHAPTER 9

I spent the first few hours of my sleepless night staring up at my ceiling and thinking about the epidemic of deaths among the older population of Goodnight. There were a handful of suspects, and it wasn't certain that the deaths were connected, even with the list of curses. What did Jenny and Joyce mean that they had been interrupted before they could carry out the curses, and should I believe them?

I sat up in bed with a jolt. "Tony Eddy needs to be warned," I said out loud. But my phone said it was two o'clock. The middle of the night. I would have to wait until morning to warn him. Abbott and Costello's heads perked up, and I took them for a long walk in the forest to use up some more time. Insomnia can be lonely. I do have to admit that I paused at Boone's door on the way out because I knew of something that could pass the time better than walking the dogs. But his lights were off. And I was totally off men.

The next morning, I was the second person in the Gazette office after Klee. I called Tony Eddy and warned him that he was on a cursed list.

"I'm not buying what you're selling, lady," he yelled into the phone and hung up on me. It wasn't easy being a Girl Scout. I needed to see him in person before he wound up dead like the rest of them. Somehow, my car was returned home, but I couldn't drive it without a key. According to Goodnight Garage, a new car fob cost two hundred dollars, which was approximately one thousand peanut butter and jelly sandwiches.

"Klee, may I borrow your car?" I asked her.

She laughed. "Good one, Matilda. Great sense of humor."

Silas walked in and plopped down in his chair. He jiggled his mouse and started typing furiously on his keyboard. "That poor bastard Adam Beatman's in real hot water, boss," Silas said. "Doesn't he know not to talk to journalists?"

"What did he say?" I asked.

"All about how much he hated his stepmother and about her spending his retirement. Idiot. Now I have to write it all up, and he's going to go to jail because of it. Adam's on my bowling team. We'll never get to the championships now."

"You bowl?"

I couldn't imagine Silas moving his body that much. His cholesterol level must have been sky high, and I worried that any movement at all would shift the cholesterol in his arteries and give him a heart attack.

"I'm the official scorekeeper. Reporters don't bowl."

"Do you think Adam killed his stepmother?" I asked.

"I think he could have killed her, but not with vaginal soap."

It was the same thing that Boone had told me.

Silas leaned forward. "You still working on that list?" he asked me, softly. I nodded. "That Tony Eddy guy? The retired washer dryer repairman? He worked on all of the other dead folks' washers. Leonard, Stella, and Margaret. Might be an avenue to go down, boss."

"How did you find out?"

"As long as there's shoe leather left on my Hush Puppies, I never stop. Just like the free press. We never stop. You can imprison us, but we never stop. You can censor us, but we never stop. You can pay us next to nothing, but we never stop."

Silas really loved the free press.

"May I borrow your car?" I asked him.

"No. I've got back-to-back stories today. Quint gave Fifi a nervous breakdown, and she locked herself in the Giraffe Museum. She won't stop hugging the stuffed version of Daisy the Giraffe in the display."

While he wrote his story, I searched through the database of runaway girls again. There were thousands of them. I figured it was going to take me weeks to find her, if I found her at all.

And then I found her about five minutes into my search.

Devyn Jones. Eighteen years old. From West Texas. She barely looked like her picture. She was thinner now, and the smiling, bright-eyed girl staring back at me from the monitor was little like the scarily thin girl who appeared to me in the canyon and at the river. But it was her, all right.

I called Amos and told him that I found another girl. "I'll be right there," he said and hung up.

Amos arrived a couple of minutes later, at about the same time that Boone walked in and almost made me swallow my tongue. "What're you wearing?" I asked him.

"A suit. All of my regular clothes are dirty, so

I'm stuck with this."

He was a GQ model in a suit. George Clooney wished he looked like Boone in a suit.

"What an asshole," Amos said under his breath. "Did you have to wear a tie, too?"

"It's part of the suit, asshole," Boone told him, running a hand down his tie, smoothing it. Holy cow, he was hot. Even hotter than when he was wet and mostly naked.

"Like you put on a suit because it's laundry day," Amos growled, looking from Boone to me and back again. "You know, the Cook-off might not happen this year after what happened," he said, as if to tell the world to lay off him because he was having a bad time.

"What the hell is going on?" Klee demanded. "This is a place of business. I'm trying to format the story on the shit falling from the sky. So, stay professional, people, or leave."

I gave Amos the rundown on the second dead girl and showed him the picture. It was obvious he didn't want to believe me, but he took down the information anyway and promised to contact her family.

"Can you give me a ride?" I asked him. "My car key went down the rapids."

"I'll take you," Boone announced, standing up.

"I got nothing else to do but wait for my clothes. You know, unless you want to take her, asshole."

I sighed. They had a strange relationship. They hated each other, yet they were worried to step on the other's toes when it came to me. I wasn't sure if either of them were truly interested in me. Amos had seemed to be, but I couldn't compete with his lost love. And as for Boone, he was a mystery.

"No, you take her," Amos said softly and walked out of the office, his cowboy boots making a racket on the wood floor.

Silas looked up from his computer. "What's going on? Is something going on?"

"I'm giving Matilda a ride," Boone explained.

Klee snorted, and that just about said it all.

"Did you bring my car back?" I asked Boone as we drove away.

"It wasn't hard."

It was the second time that he had retrieved my car for me from the wilds outside of Goodnight. I tried not to focus on his chivalry too much because it was distracting me from what was important. I had found the second girl, and now I had her name. I was one step closer to finding the monster who was abducting and murdering blond girls in Goodnight. I felt like Wonder Woman, like Superman.

"Tony's a good guy," he continued, moving on from talking about my car. "But there's something off about him. Loner. Quiet. Something not all there about him."

That description could have fit half of the town. We arrived at Tony's house a few minutes later. It was a two-story adobe, and Boone parked on the street. I rang the doorbell and eyed Boone from the corner of my eye. In my jeans and sweater, I was definitely underdressed next to him. I could tell that he knew how good he looked in his suit because he had a perpetual smile on his face, like he felt proud of himself.

Nobody answered the door, so I rang the bell again and knocked. "Maybe he's out repairing a dryer," I suggested.

"He's retired."

"Do you know how to pick locks?" I asked.

"How about we come back later? We could go out to lunch."

"Huh?" Was he asking me out on a date? He was dressed like a man ready to go on a date. I felt myself blush, and I fell against the door, and it opened with a creak.

"Oh, no," Boone moaned. "This isn't good. A

creaking open door. You opened the portal to hell again."

"Maybe he forgot to lock up."

I took a step, but Boone put his arm out and blocked me. "Nuh-uh. I'll go in first."

He went inside, and I quickly followed. It turned out that Tony was a hoarder, and there had to be cats around, because it smelled like cat pee. I covered my nose and mouth with my sweater. Boone and I carefully made our way through old newspapers, clothes, appliances, and trash.

"I don't understand this," I said. "I get not wanting to wash the dishes for one night, but this? I don't get it."

"I've never been here before, and I never want to be here again."

The kitchen was even worse. The cats had used it as one giant litter box, and there was cat feces all over the place. "I'm going to throw up," I said. "I don't care if Tony was cursed by the sisters. He's already cursed, as far as I'm concerned."

"Matilda, look over there," Boone said.

"Where?"

"The floor by the sink."

"Is that?"

"Tony Eddy. Yes."

He was lying on the floor by the sink, a spilled glass of water by his head. He was dead. We could tell he was dead without checking.

"I can't believe I'm seeing another dead body," I said. "It's like I'm going for a world record or something."

"Portal to hell."

"He hung up on me an hour ago," I said.

"It looks like he was sick. Check out his skin. His hair."

"Like he was poisoned?" I asked.

Boone shrugged. "Murder's your expertise, not mine."

We waited around for Amos and the coroner, who crossed himself when he saw me. I was getting a reputation as the angel of death. Once they arrived and had the situation under control, Boone and I got in his truck and headed back to my house.

"Are you going to the funeral?" Boone asked.

"Which one?"

"Margaret's. It starts in thirty minutes. Bernard called and invited me this morning. It might be a good place to pick up clues. There's going to be a big turnout. I think most folks want to see the meanest bitch in

Goodnight dead and buried."

We went home, and I changed into a black skirt and white top after eating another sandwich. Then, Boone drove me to the funeral. Sure enough, there was a big turnout. In fact, all of the suspects showed up. The crowd circled the casket, which was perched above the hole in the ground. It was a gorgeous day, not a cloud in the sky, and a perfect sixty-eight degrees. The cemetery was a large patch of green in an otherwise brown area.

Everyone said hello to Boone, but there was a lot of ignoring going on where I was concerned. I didn't blame them. I was a death magnet.

Adam Beatman was standing with his father and wife. His eyes darted around, as if he was waiting to be carted off to jail at any moment. He had bought his stepmother vaginal soap and hated her guts. Made sense. Vaginal soap wasn't exactly the gift one gave to a loved one.

Jenny and Joyce showed up with Nora. Nora caught my eye. My normally unshakable friend looked pretty freaked out, and I wondered how long she would stay in her job. Jenny and Joyce ignored me. They were too busy waving crystals around and making *woo-woo* noises. They were all kinds of shady, and I still wasn't counting out my theory that they used the curse list as a hit list to up their street cred in the psychic department.

But they did seem to be telling the truth when they said their curses got interrupted.

And then there were the VIP Tickets to Heaven. There was a good chance that the scam artist for that one was among the mourners. Perhaps he had been found out and had to silence his victims.

"Bernard's brother Ted showed up," Boone whispered to me. "He's the golden boy. He could do no wrong in Margaret's eyes."

"He didn't have to stay in a box under her bed?"

"Not the favorite son. Now he's some kind of business guy in Albuquerque."

Bernard waved at Boone. "Come on. I'll introduce you," Boone told me. He put his hand on my lower back as we walked.

"Hello there," Ted said like he hadn't eaten for weeks, and I was a Big Mac. He took my hand and brought it to his lips. *Ewww.* Ted was creepy and greasy, and I got a big rapey vibe off of him. "You're new. We don't normally get beautiful women in Goodnight except for Faye. You with Boone? You busy later? You want to go to dinner?"

Boone put his arm around my waist. "She's busy tonight, Ted."

"No problem. I'm busy, too. I have to help Bernard with the paperwork."

"Ted is letting me live in his house," Bernard said, excitedly.

"Mother left me the house, of course," Ted said. My ears pricked up, and the hair on my arms stood on end. "But Bernard will keep living there. I mean where else is he going to go?" He barked laughter until he was interrupted by the reverend, who wanted to start the ceremony.

"The plot thickens," Boone whispered in my ear. "Ted made a pretty penny off his mother's death."

The reverend completed the short service, and Nora grabbed me on her way out. "I thought the mourners were going to applaud when they put her in the ground," she said. "Everyone here hated that woman, and they had good reason. Meanest bitch in Goodnight, even though she was always nice to me. But she probably hated me anyway. She hated everybody."

Nora skipped away to catch up to her bosses, and I was left standing with Boone, thinking about Margaret and all of the deaths that had happened this week. Taken together, there didn't seem to be a rhyme or reason behind them. It was like I was trying to put together a puzzle, but either some pieces were missing, or I was actually working on more than one puzzle at a time.

"So, you and me, then?" Boone asked, waking

me up from my thoughts.

"Excuse me?"

"Dinner. You want to go with me, or should I call Ted back for you?"

"I don't think I could eat anywhere near Ted, but if you're paying, I wouldn't mind eating with you."

"Then, it's a date."

CHAPTER 10

There was a handwritten sign on the door to Goodnight Diner. *We reserve the right to refuse service to anyone with poop on their head.* Boone opened the door for me, and I walked in. The diner was busy, but it wasn't anything close to lunch traffic.

"We're closing in an hour," Adele said, greeting us. She looked like she had just run a marathon after being released from the Hanoi Hilton.

"Are you all right?" I asked her, putting my hand on her shoulder.

"Matilda, I can't watch another set of jaws chew. Haven't these people heard of intermittent fasting? Don't they ever take a break? Don't they have food at home?"

"I'm so sorry. You've been through a hard

time."

"Someone's got to open another restaurant in this town quick. I'm going to need CPR."

"Where's Morris?" Boone said, pointing toward the kitchen.

"That's Jerome. He's filling in for Morris until this calms down. Morris is preparing for the Cook-off, even though they say it might not happen now. That's just great. Another day when people will want more food from me. Morris is still working lunch, though."

Adele guided us to a booth by the window. She handed us menus, but she informed us that they only had waffles and BLTs left. I ordered the waffles, and Boone got a BLT. Adele left to place our orders, and for the first time since I met Boone, we were sitting alone, face to face, with nothing to distract us but ourselves.

I tried to swallow, but it was difficult, and I made a gulping noise. He was a very handsome man. I knew a little about what was considered a perfectly formed face. The distance from the hairline to the top of the nose must be equidistant to the length of the nose equidistant from the bottom of the nose to the chin. He had it all. Beautiful, perfect symmetry messed up by a thin scar that ran crooked along his chin, like the Snake River itself. His face was deeply tanned with remnants of sunburn on his forehead and nose. Obviously, he had been somewhere outside under the sun while he was away. His thick hair had been bleached by the sun, and I put my hands in my lap to stop myself from running my fingers through it.

Damned chemistry.

Damned Goodnight men.

It was hard to tear my eyes away from studying his face, but after a while, I relaxed enough to realize that he was studying me as much as I was studying him. His mouth turned up in a smile.

"So…" he began and smiled wider.

"Here's your waters," Adele said, putting two glasses down on our table. "Do you mind if I sit with you?"

"No. Go ahead," I said after a moment's pause. She sat down and took a deep breath, but the door opened, and she was up again.

"So…" Boone repeated when she was gone.

"This isn't a date," I interrupted. What was I saying? "I'm still married. My divorce isn't final, so I'm not ready for a relationship." What the hell was I saying? Why did my mouth keep moving?

"I understand. How do you know I want a relationship? Maybe I just want a meal."

"Oh. Well…"

"Or maybe I just want to sleep with you."

I coughed, and my face grew hot. "You…I…"

"Or maybe I find you amusing, how you fall into mysteries and work your way out of them, like a clumsy Jessica Fletcher."

"You think I'm like Jessica Fletcher?" I asked hopefully.

"Yes. You look just like her."

"What?"

He touched my cheek, running his thumb down my cheekbone and across my jawline. "Maybe not exactly like Jessica Fletcher."

Our eyes locked, and warmth pooled in my lower body. I felt myself melting, and I was pretty sure that I would say yes to anything he asked.

Luckily, Adele came back with our food and sat down at the table. "Go ahead and eat," she told us. "Don't worry. It's okay. I can take watching you eat. I've been doing it nonstop for days."

"You really need a break," I told her.

Nora came in and sat down with us, scooting Boone over.

"I can't go home. I told the hubby to watch the kids," she said.

"What's wrong?" I asked.

"I quit my job. I guess I'll have to go back to the bank. I was hoping to get out from under our debts, but…you got anything to drink, Adele?"

"I'm lucky I still have water."

My friends were down and exhausted. "I have three bottles of champagne at home," I announced. I had been saving them for when my divorce was finalized, but my friends were worth it. "And I can get snacks from the store. You want to do a girls' night?"

Nora and Adele brightened considerably. "That sounds wonderful," Adele said.

Nora looked at Boone and then at me. "Hey, what's going on here? Why is Boone wearing a suit?"

"It's laundry day," he said.

"Why's he wearing a suit with you, Matilda?" Adele asked, catching on.

"My car key fell down the rapids. Boone has been driving me." Adele and Nora exchanged a look. "Well, he has!" I insisted.

Nora rolled her eyes, and Adele pursed her lips. I took a bite of my waffle.

"Why did you quit that job?" Adele asked Nora.

"Those witches cursed me when they caught me snooping. I'll never use vaginal soap again."

Boone choked on his BLT, and Nora slapped his back.

"Beware of high places, too," I told Nora.

Nora and Adele followed us home, and we called Faye to join us. Boone closed himself up in his part of the house. I opened a bottle of champagne and popped a big bowl of popcorn. We sat at the kitchen table, and Abbott and Costello lay on the floor underneath it.

"I'm going to quit, too," Faye announced.

"No, you're not," Nora told her. "You need that job. Norton needs the extra cash to get a new UFO on his store's roof."

"He's got his eye on a real beauty, imported all the way from Jakarta," Faye agreed.

"I feel responsible for you losing your job," I said to Nora.

"Are you kidding? I quit that job. That was my decision. You're only responsible for me getting cursed."

She gave me a sloppy hug. She had three glasses of champagne in her, and she was feeling no pain. Adele and Faye were blotto, too.

"Maybe you can catch some of those giraffes," Faye suggested to Nora. "Thirty giraffes would net you sixty thousand dollars. That would keep you afloat for a while."

"Those are the wiliest giraffes on the planet.

Nobody has been able to get one," Adele said. "I hear the stories all day long every day in the diner. My eaters have tried everything to make a buck catching those giraffes."

"How hard can it be to catch a giraffe?" Nora asked, as if she was thinking about making a few bucks that way. "They got those long bodies. Long necks. You could throw a lasso and catch one real easy. You pretty much couldn't miss. Am I right?"

"Do you know how to lasso?" I asked.

"No, but how hard is it to learn? You got any rope, Matilda?"

"I have rope in my truck," Faye said. "You want me to get it?"

"Sure. I could practice here. You got anything for me to lasso, Matilda? Anything really tall with a long neck?"

"Uh…" I said.

Faye got the rope and tied it into a crude lasso. "Start with the chair," Adele suggested.

"A chair is nothing like a giraffe," Faye said and hiccoughed. "Try and lasso me." She put her hand up in the air. "See? My arm is like a giraffe's neck."

"I think giraffes are taller," I said, uneasy at the prospect of Nora drunk lassoing anything in my house.

"They're not taller if you're uphill," Faye said.

"That's true!" Adele said. "You're so smart, Faye."

"Here I go," Nora announced and swung the rope over her head in a big circle. *Crash*! First she broke the ceiling light. *Crash*! Then, she knocked the champagne bottle off the table. *Crash!* And finally, she sent the teapot on the stove flying into the closed window, cracking it in half.

"That was pretty good," Faye said. "You've got good form. You came pretty close to my arm."

"Yeah, try again," Adele said. "You got to get to a point where it's muscle memory."

"Like farting?" Nora asked and raised the lasso over her head again.

"Maybe you should try it outside," I suggested.

"It's dark outside," Nora said.

"Yeah, that's for when you're really good at it," Adele said. "Like a ninja. Ninjas do shit in the dark."

"Do ninjas catch giraffes?" Nora asked.

"Tons of them," Adele said.

"Try again," Faye said, stretching her arm high.

"Oh God," I moaned. The dogs cowered under the table.

Nora lifted the rope up above her head and swung it around harder and faster, but with the alcohol running through her veins, she lost her balance and fell back against the cabinet. The cabinet doors swung open, and all of my salad plates fell crashing to the floor.

I would never be able to eat salad again.

"Holy cow!" Nora yelled and tried to right herself, flinging the rope forward, like it was a whip. It landed with a loud *crack!* on Faye's face, and she screamed and flew backward into the pantry, where she took down the coffee, bread, a pound of sugar, and all of my spices. The dogs went running into the pantry after her in hopes of finding stuff on the floor to eat.

Nora, Adele, and I checked on Faye. "I guess it's harder to lasso than I thought," Adele said. "Maybe you have the wrong kind of rope."

"I got the nylon kind in my truck," Faye said, brightly, as we helped her up.

An hour later, my three friends were asleep. Nora and Faye were zonked out on my bed, and Adele was on the couch. Of course, I was wide awake as usual, which was good because I had a lot of cleaning up to do.

I was duct taping a coffeemaker that Nora's rope had knocked to the floor on her third lasso try when the house phone rang. I ran to answer it before it could wake up my friends.

"Hello?"

"You bitch," the voice on the other end sneered.

"Excuse me?"

"You heard me." I froze and hugged myself with my free arm. I did hear him. I knew the voice, but I didn't know how he was calling me. Especially how he was calling me in the middle of the night. I had a restraining order against him, and the prison didn't allow phone calls at night, as far as I knew.

"What do you want, Rockwell?" It was my husband. The husband I wanted to be my ex-husband. Had he broken out of prison? I put my hands against the window and tried to see out, but it was pitch black outside.

"You'll never get a divorce. You're trying to ruin my life."

"You're crazy! You're loony tunes! You're in jail for life. You're never getting out."

"I want my inheritance, Matilda. It's mine. You're not going to divorce me."

Rockwell's inheritance was contingent on staying married for five years. But why was he still so obsessed with his inheritance when he would never have a chance to spend it?

"I'm hanging up, Rockwell. You can't stop the divorce, no matter how much you try."

"Oh, yeah? You think I can't reach you over there in New Mexico? You think I don't have eyes on you right this second?"

Icy dread crept up my body like a virus taking over my system. "I don't believe you," I lied.

"Oh, yeah? I know you have two dogs now. You want them to stay healthy? It would be easy to slip them something and watch them go bye-bye."

"You wouldn't dare," I said, fighting back tears. I had grown close to my adopted dogs, and I couldn't bear the idea of them getting hurt or worse.

"No divorce, Matilda. Call your lawyer. Or else."

The line went dead. I looked at the receiver for a moment, like I expected Rockwell to climb out of it. I was gripped with fear, sure that he had escaped and sure that my life was in danger. I hung up the phone as quietly as I could. Tip-toeing into my bedroom, I got the crowbar I kept next to my bed and crept outside to look around and make sure that my ex-husband wasn't lying in wait for me or my dogs.

I held the crowbar like I was batting cleanup at the World Series. Trying to drum up courage was hard because if I was totally honest with myself, I was scared shitless of my ex-husband.

There was no moon out tonight, but there were plenty of stars, and I could make out the courtyard without turning on the lights. The dogs were still fast asleep inside, and so I was all alone.

"You can do this," I told myself. "Just check the perimeter." I walked around the courtyard, finding nothing. "See? He's in San Quentin. Nobody escapes from San Quentin."

Feeling slightly less frightened, I walked gingerly out of the gate and went left to circle the house. Out of nowhere, strong hands gripped my shoulders. It was him! He did escape! I swung wildly with the crowbar and made contact.

I hope I killed you, you son of a bitch.

CHAPTER 11

"Sonofabitch!"

Uh-oh. I recognized that voice. "Boone?" I asked. Oops.

"I think you broke my arm," he croaked, like he couldn't believe the words were coming out of his mouth.

"I'm sure I didn't break your arm."

"I'm sure it's not supposed to hang at this angle. In fact, it's not supposed to hang at any angle. It's my forearm!"

I squinted through the darkness. Boone was lying on the ground, holding his arm to his chest. He was wearing boxer briefs and nothing more.

"Why did you sneak up on me?" I demanded. "You sneak up on a woman at night, you should expect to get your arm broken with a crowbar."

"Ha! I told you it was broken! Is that what you hit me with? A crowbar? Are you psychotic?"

"I use it for protection. Would you have rather I shot you with a gun? I don't believe in guns."

"You don't believe they exist, or you draw the line at maiming your renters, not shooting them?"

"What were you doing, sneaking up on me half-naked in the middle of the night?" I demanded.

"You woke me up with your skulking around. I was sleeping, and I put on boxers before I came out. You know, with you and the portal of hell and all, I thought you might need some help. What're you doing out here?"

I gnawed on the inside of my cheek and tried to think up a reasonable explanation, but all I could think of was the fact that he slept in the buff. "I was checking the perimeter," I said, finally.

"Why? Are you Rambo?"

"I thought my soon-to-be ex-husband might have escaped from San Quentin and was stalking me." Boone rocked his head side to side, as if he was weighing something. "What? What is it?"

"No. Nothing."

"What? Just spit it out. You think I'm crazy or have opened another portal to hell. Just tell me."

"It's nothing, really. It's just that I was thinking that imagining your ex-husband was stalking you was a step up from talking to dead people."

"Very funny," I said. I swung the crowbar onto my shoulder. "I'm going to bed. Good night."

"Hold on. Aren't you forgetting something?"

"I'll check the rest of the perimeter when the sun comes up," I said.

"No, not that, Mother Teresa. You broke my arm. You have to take me to the hospital."

"Oh. That."

I helped him up, and we went toward his part of the house so that he could get dressed. He opened his door, and I paused on the threshold. "Aren't you coming in?" he asked.

"You're letting me in?"

"I need help to get dressed. You're probably not aware of this because I'm a studly manly man, but my arm is *broken*. It hurts like a motherfucker. At least one big bone in my arm is broken and poking my skin. If I had slightly less testosterone running through my body, I would cry like a baby. Already, I'm fantasizing about morphine in a really big and disturbing way. So, yes, I need help getting dressed."

Wow, for someone in a lot of pain, he sure could talk. "So just to be clear, you're letting me in?" I asked.

"Just get in here and zip my goddamned pants for me."

I stepped inside. It was a disaster area, not at all inhabitable. There were rocks everywhere. Shelves and shelves of them and a long table in the middle of the room covered with them. "What the hell?" I asked.

"Oh, yeah. It's messy, but not dirty. All this goes with the job."

I followed him into his small bedroom. "What job?"

"Why are you so interested in what I do for a living?"

"You make a living?"

He gestured with his head. "I have clean jeans in the basket there."

I helped him put on his jeans, and he tucked part of a shirt in his back pocket because it was too difficult to put it on. He tossed me the keys to his truck.

"I need to put my crowbar away and get my purse," I said.

"The purse thing, again? You don't have a cell phone anymore. Ditto the keys. Why do you need your purse?"

"My driver's license is in there. It got wet, but it's still a driver's license. Be quiet when we go in. The girls are sleeping."

Sweat was beading on his forehead and his upper lip, and I could tell that he was in a lot of pain, but his arm looked fine to me. We walked into my kitchen, and I got my purse.

"What the hell happened here?" Boone asked, looking at the damage that Nora had done with her lasso.

"Nora's going to try and make money capturing giraffes."

"There was a giraffe in here?"

"It's a long story. I'll tell you in the emergency room. What a waste of time. Your arm isn't broken."

"Matilda, my arm is broken."

I put my hands on my hips. "Your arm isn't broken. I'll bet you a million dollars that your arm isn't broken."

"You're sure it's broken?" I asked the doctor, as he put a cast on Boone's arm while Boone sat up in bed.

The doctor nodded. "Spiral fracture. Real nasty. I almost threw up. I'll be glad when this puppy is fully cast and I don't have to look at it."

Boone stuck his tongue out at me. "Neener neener. Told you so," he sang.

"Did you give him a painkiller?" I asked the doctor.

"I gave him the good juice," he said and high-fived Boone. "He's not going to feel any pain for a good long time. Least I could do. Boone and I go way back."

"Doc used to sell crystal meth under the bleachers during lunch," Boone said, smiling. "That's how he got his name. Doc. And now he's really a doc. So..."

"Boone wasn't one of my customers at school, but we were on the same baseball team," the doctor explained. "Boone is a great pitcher. Well, he used to be. I don't think he'll ever pitch again after this."

We left the hospital, and I helped Boone into the passenger seat of his truck. He was flying high, like he was at Studio 54 in the seventies.

"You know, we're in Tony Eddy's neighborhood," I said. "Amos has blocked me at every turn to really investigate these deaths. He's always there, not letting me snoop the way I want. The sun isn't up, yet. Would you mind if we went to Tony's house and gave it a good going over?"

"You're pretty," Boone said, and he slumped against the window and started to snore.

The sun was starting to come up when I parked in front of Tony's house. I nudged Boone awake, and unfortunately, he was already starting to sober up.

"What are we doing here?"

"I told you. We're investigating."

"But I have a boo-boo arm."

"Seriously? What happened to the studly manly man?"

"I have instant hot chocolate at home. That would really hit the spot," he whined.

"Maybe Tony has instant hot chocolate, too."

"I'm not eating or drinking anything from his house. Are you trying to kill me?"

He was right. I had forgotten how disgusting Tony's house was. We broke in through an open back door. The cats had been rescued and taken away, but it still smelled like they were there.

"How do people live like this?" Boone asked.

"Tony's dead, so let's not worry about it."

The dawn was breaking, and Tony's house didn't look any better than it had the first time I had seen it. A little path had been cleared where the paramedics and sheriffs got through to work on Tony. I was putting on a brave, I-don't-care-about-filth face, but my OCD, love-of-all-things-clean-and-organized self was dying to dig into the mess and clean it all up. It was practically killing me not to throw everything away and scrub all the surfaces down with Pine-Sol.

"What're we looking for?" Boone asked.

"I don't know. A VIP Ticket to Heaven, maybe."

"A what?"

I tapped the tip of my nose with my finger, as I thought. "We're probably going to need to go into his bedroom."

"Oh God. I can only imagine what he's got in there."

His bedroom was nasty. Worse than any dorm room I had ever seen. He had no sheet on his bed, and there were cat feces in the room, too. Dirt and garbage was piled high in every direction.

"You think we're going to get a staph infection, or am I being paranoid?" I asked Boone.

"I'm going to bathe in bleach when I get out of here."

"Search in his nightstand," I ordered Boone.

"No way. I know what's in my nightstand, and it's disgusting enough. And I'm normal. I can't imagine what's in his nightstand."

"You're just looking for this. At least I think you are," I said, taking out the two water-damaged heaven tickets from my purse. I had dried them with a hairdryer, and they were mostly intact, at least enough to make out what they were.

"What the hell is a VIP Ticket to Heaven?" Boone asked.

"Exactly."

He opened the nightstand drawer with the toe of his shoe, and sure enough, there were a lot of sticky, disgusting things in it. But right on top was another golden ticket framed in blue wings. "Eureka," I said. "Bingo. Voila. There she blows. The plot may be thicker, but my Jessica Fletcher nose has got major talent."

"It smells like cats peed on possum corpses, and then Ozzy Osbourne bit their heads off and threw up all over everything," Boone said.

"Duly noted. We can leave now."

I put the ticket in my purse. It was hard to leave the house messy. I generally needed order in my life. I remembered that I had all kinds of lasso damage at my house to clean up, and the realization made me itch.

"You hungry?" I asked Boone when we returned to Tony's kitchen.

"Starving. Maybe we could take a road trip and get pancakes? I'm not sure I can brave the diner again."

My stomach growled at the thought of a big pancake breakfast with bacon and coffee. "Let's do it."

"It's a date. Another one," Boone said and smiled wide.

"We've never been on a date," I insisted.

"Okay. Play it that way. I'm a patient man. I…wait a minute. That's odd." Boone walked around me and crouched down. He studied the floor. "This cabinet moved."

"What do you mean? It moved just now? Like from rats or something?"

"No, I mean it's been moved repeatedly. It's hard to tell because the floor is filthy, but it's like a Hogan's Heroes kind of secret door." He stood and faced me. "This might be good, or it might be the most disgusting thing we ever see, and we'll be scarred forever. It's up to you if we try to open it. You decide."

"How do we get the secret door open?"

Boone opened it with one hand. It opened up to a staircase that went down to a dark room. "Holy shit. This is like a scary movie," I said. "Rule number one in a scary movie: Don't go in the cellar."

"Does that mean you want me to go down first?" Boone asked.

I nodded. He stepped down and found a light switch. Light flooded the room below, and we walked quickly down the rest of the way.

"Sonofabitch," Boone said.

The room was filled with television monitors, at least ten of them on one wall. There was a desk in the center, piled high with paper and a keyboard, and on the wall behind it were photos. A whole wall of photos.

"That's Stella," I said, pointing at one of the pictures. "I recognize her from her wake."

"Margaret," Boone said, pointing at another picture. "Sonofabitch."

Not only had Tony worked on the washers and dryers of all of the dead people, but he had stalked them. "These pictures of them were all taken in their homes," I noted.

Boone pushed some buttons on the keyboard, and the monitors came to life. On one screen, I saw Bernard and Ted in Margaret's house. Bernard was standing over Ted in his pajamas, serving him his breakfast. It was video in real time.

"Tony was spying on all of them," I said. "Why?"

"Because he was crazy, I'm thinking."

"There's the witches' mansion on that monitor," I said, pointing. "But they're not dead."

"So you think Tony Eddy killed all those people? But who killed him?"

It was a good question. "Maybe he killed himself after he killed those people." But the theory didn't seem to fit for me. The tickets to heaven were knocking at my brain, telling me that they were important. And what about the curses? How did they fit in?

"Everything's so confused. Chaotic," I said. "I wonder if it's supposed to be, if it's designed to make us turn in every direction."

"Us?"

"I think we need to go back to the beginning, to where it all began."

"After the pancakes," Boone insisted. "I'll pay, but the least you can do after breaking my arm is to take me to eat pancakes."

"You snuck up on me!"

"You were skulking!"

We drove to a breakfast place about halfway between Goodnight and Santa Fe. Boone waved to a bunch of people he knew when we entered. "C'mon," he said to me and took my hand. At first, I didn't know where he was taking me, but then I saw him. Adam Beatman. Suspended deputy sheriff. Suspected stepmother killer. Verified vaginal soap gift giver. Adam was sitting alone in a center booth. He was sipping a cup of coffee and looked up just as Boone slipped into the seat across from him and patted the vinyl for me to sit next to him.

"Hey there, Adam, how's it hangin'?" Boone said.

"Hey there, Boone. Glad to see you made it out of the wilderness without getting eaten." His looked in my direction. "I can't talk to you people anymore," he said to me. "Silas kicked me in the balls with that last interview. My ass is going to fry in the electric chair."

"Totally off the record. This is just a social call," I said in my best Carl Bernstein voice.

The waitress came with Adam's breakfast, and Boone and I ordered. When the waitress left again, Adam salted his food and sized us up.

"You two a couple? I thought Amos was going after the new girl. I heard he cooked for her." Adam said.

I gulped and squirmed in my seat. Amos had cooked for me. Twice. But he was definitely not romantically interested in me anymore. That ship had sailed. Or had it?

"We're not a couple. I'm a journalist," I said, as if that meant anything. Did it mean anything? I didn't know. I had broken out into a sweat, and I gulped down Adam's glass of water.

"Hey Adam," Boone said, ignoring the couple question. "Tell us why you bought your stepmother vaginal soap."

CHAPTER 12

"That? I'm never going to live that down," Adam growled. "What do I know? One of her friends said to get it for her for her birthday. I had to get her something, or my father would have skinned me alive. She said women like that sort of thing. I should have known she was lying to me."

"Who?" I asked.

"Margaret Marshall, the meanest bitch in Goodnight."

I gasped and leaned back in my seat. "You bought it from her?"

"No, she just told me what to get. That's all. Why? You think the bitch offed my stepmother? That would be wonderful. You got any proof?"

"No. Why would she kill her? And if she did,

maybe you killed Margaret to avenge your stepmother."

Adam laughed and pointed his fork at me. "Good one. I like your sense of humor."

"Do you have any idea who wanted your stepmother killed?" I asked him.

"Who knows? I didn't know her friends, but she did hang around those witches an awful lot. So did Margaret, actually. Huh. I forgot about that. That's another link between the two. Hey, Amos!" Adam called and waved his hand.

I turned around to see Sheriff Amos Goodnight walk in. He was wearing his usual uniform of boots, jeans, a button-down shirt, and a cowboy hat. He wasn't pleased when he saw me sitting with Adam, and he was even less pleased when he noticed Boone.

"What did you do to your arm, asshole?" he asked Boone.

"What's it to you, asshole?" Boone shot back.

I sighed. I didn't have any siblings, and for the first time in my life, I was happy about it. Boone and Amos were constantly at each other's throats. "Why can't you two get along?" I asked.

"They used to be best friends," Adam said, taking a sip of his coffee. "Then, you know what happened."

"What happened?" I asked.

"Matilda, I'm glad you're here. I got something to tell you," Amos said, changing the conversation. Boone rolled his eyes. The waitress arrived with our food. "It won't take a minute," Amos added.

I slipped out of the booth and followed Amos to the back of the restaurant by the bathrooms. "Deep background," he started.

"Silas is going to kill me. Nobody does deep background with him."

Amos arched an eyebrow. "Deep background. Silas will get this information later, but I thought with all the snooping you're doing, you might need to know first."

"How do you know I'm snooping?"

He arched his other eyebrow.

"Okay, I'm snooping," I said. "And fine to the deep background as long as you tell Silas soon."

"He'll know when the report comes out, which will happen in a couple days, but I thought you'd like to know. Leonard Shetland died of a heart attack."

I was sort of stunned, and I took a step back, hitting the wall. "You mean the poison gave him a heart attack?"

"What poison?"

"The poison that killed him."

Amos ran a hand down his face. "There was no

poison. He had a heart attack. Natural causes."

"I'm confused. Who murdered him?"

"God. God murdered him. It was natural causes. You understand natural causes? He died of a heart attack. You know, he ate a lot of cheese."

"He wrote the letter and then he dropped dead of a heart attack?" I asked.

"Died in his sleep. Lucky bastard."

He wrote the letter and then dropped dead. How was that possible? Did coincidences like that exist in the world? "Well, that makes one less murder," I said. "We're down to three."

"Two. We're calling Margaret's death an accident. By the way, it looks like Tony was poisoned with the same thing as Stella."

"He used vaginal soap?" I asked.

"No. It was in his eye drops. Tony had glaucoma."

Eye drops. Vaginal soap. It was like the local pharmacist was knocking folks off. "Thank you for the deep background."

"You better get to your food before it gets cold. I just stopped by for a cup of coffee. The diner's a mess, and I need caffeine if I'm going to finally get Fifi to leave that damned Friends of Daisy the Giraffe Home for Abused Wildlife."

"Did she give up trying to save the giraffes? What happened to Quint?"

"I don't know about Fifi. Strange woman. She keeps going on about needing a bigger boat. We let her stay the night in the museum to see if that calmed her. Meanwhile, no one's seen Quint in a while."

"I saw him at the river when you were fishing."

"No one's seen him since then," Amos said. "I hope a giraffe ate him."

I turned to go back to the booth, but a niggling guilt worked at me, and I figured one good deed deserved another. I turned back to Amos.

"This is on deep background," I began.

"It doesn't go that way, from journalist to law enforcement. It's the other way around. Law enforcement to journalist."

"Just work with me here, will you?"

Amos sighed and put three fingers up in a Boy Scout promise. "Fine. Deep background."

"Go back to Tony Eddy's house. There's a secret door in the kitchen that looks like a cabinet. It'll take you to a cellar. There's stuff in the cellar you'll want to look at."

"What stuff?"

"My food's getting cold," I said.

Amos grabbed my arm and pulled me back to

him. "Be careful, Trouble."

"I'm careful. Boone has been with me."

"No, I mean be careful of Boone."

As I walked back to the booth, my mind was swimming. Maybe Leonard's letter was a hint, and he was actually the killer? There were so many suspects now that I could start a baseball team with them. But now the one link between all the victims was clear. Jenny and Joyce.

Boone and I ate with Adam, and by the time we were done, Boone was fading fast. I decided to take him home before I did any more snooping. I put him to bed with a cup of instant hot chocolate and returned to my side of the house, where my dogs were waiting for me.

They danced around me, begging for their breakfast. "I'm so sorry I'm late," I told them. I scooped dog food out of the airtight container and poured it in their bowls and gave them fresh water. My friends had left while I was away, and they had cleaned the house. Even the window was fixed, and the food in the pantry had been replaced.

Wow, you get three women together, you can change the world.

There was a message from Faye left on the

kitchen table. *Sorry for the mess. And sorry I've left you in the lurch. I'll fix the hole in the floor on Sunday. BTW, fed the dogs their breakfast. Love, Faye.*

"You liars," I told the dogs. "Faye fed you already. You ate two meals. You're con artists, just like the ticket to heaven guy and the witches." They looked up at me with big smiles on their faces. It was impossible to be upset with them. I took them for a walk in the forest before stopping by the Gazette office.

"Someone saw Bernard Marshall toss his mother off the cliff," Jack announced when I walked in the door.

"You're kidding," I said.

"I need a thousand words on the Cook-off troubles!" Klee ordered Jack.

"But Klee…" Jack whined, sounding his age. "I wanna write about Bernard offing his mom. I've been looking up all kinds of synonyms for bitch and heinous and bloody in the thesaurus."

Klee stood. She was a beautiful, stately woman. Today she was wearing a long, multi-colored woven skirt and a white shirt with a gorgeous woven scarf draped around her neck several times. Her long black hair was loose down her back, and she wasn't wearing a drop of makeup.

"The Cook-off is the biggest event in this town.

It brings in folks from all corners of Goodnight and beyond. And now everything's fucked up," Klee announced, making Jack gasp in shock. "Yes, you heard me right. F.U.C.K.ed up. That's big news, and it's a complicated story. So, that means only you or Silas can do it." Here she shot me a look like I was wasting air and space in the world. "So, get to it. I've got a call in to Silas to pick up the eyewitness to the Bernard story."

"But Klee..." Jack whined, but he was shot down immediately by her imperious stare. "Fine. Hey Matilda, you want to give me a ride to Mabel's?"

"Sure. I have the keys to Boone's truck."

I had never been to Mabel's house, so Jack gave me directions as I drove. It turned out that Mabel lived a little higher in the mountains than I did, right above the Giraffe Museum. Her house was a three-story adobe mansion with a six-car detached garage, which we passed as we drove up the long driveway.

"All of this is her land," Jack explained. "She owns half the town, you know. Bought it up from the Goodnight family. There's a lot of fighting about that at the dinner table during the holidays."

"I wonder why she bought here in Goodnight."

"She's sort of crazy. She thinks that Goodnight

is going to be the next Santa Fe. She keeps trying, but ain't nobody here thinks that's going to happen."

There were five cars parked near the front door, and just as we got there, Jenny and Joyce were getting out of theirs and walking up to the house. Holy cow. The witches.

"Do you mind if I go in with you?" I asked Jack. "I promise not to step on your toes."

"That'll be fun. We'll be like Woodward and Bernstein."

Jenny and Joyce had already gone in by the time we rang the doorbell. A servant opened the door and walked us into a great room which was almost as great as Jenny and Joyce's. The house was decorated in New Mexico chic. Lots of colors and rugs. I heard Mabel before I saw her.

"I'll sue your ass!" she was yelling. "Or I'll stab you in the eye! Someone give me a knife so I can stab her in the eye!"

"It's not my fault, Mabel. Lisa was in charge of the posters," a woman pleaded.

The servant stopped walking, and Jack and I stopped behind her. Mabel was seated at the head of a long dining table, and about fifteen others—all terrified—sat around it, too. There was a large poster on an easel behind her.

Chile Pecker Cock Off, it said in big red letters with a long, phallic chile pepper beneath it. Jack snickered next to me.

"Maybe no one will notice," someone said.

"You mean a blind person? A blind person won't notice?" Mabel was shrieking, and her face was bright red. If I had a cell phone, I would have called the paramedics, because she was about to blow.

"It's kind of funny, if you think about it," another woman said. "It might be cute, get people talking about the Cook-off.

"Talking about it?" Mabel shrieked even louder. "About the Pecker Cock Off?"

Jack was scribbling furiously in his reporter's notebook. He had pages of notes already. I was peeking at them when he elbowed me. "She's looking at you," he whispered.

I looked up. Sure enough, Mabel's eyes were lasering in on me. "What the hell are you doing here?" she demanded.

I turned around, but nobody was behind me. I pointed at my chest. "Me?" I asked.

"You wrote that libelous piece of garbage about my tea party raves, and now they've been closed down. You're the reason the town is in the toilet. I'm working against a bunch of idiots, sabotaging me at every turn."

I might have been seeing things, but I could have sworn I saw smoke come out of her ears.

"I thought I wrote a nice story about the tea party raves," I said, my voice a dead ringer for Fifi's.

"You wrote all about the seizures and the convulsions. They shut me down because of it. Like I can help it if perfectly normal strobe disco balls with a multi-colored flash make certain folks have seizures."

"I didn't write about the seizures," I said.

"Liar!"

Jack elbowed me, again. "Red lines," he muttered under his breath. Rewrites. Oh, yes. They rewrote my story to make it better. And now I was being blamed.

"Can we get back to the Cook-off?" a man at the table asked impatiently.

"You mean the Cock Off?" another man asked, and the table erupted in hysterics, except for Mabel. Jack continued to write in his notebook.

Mabel threw a pad of paper, a pen, and two posters. And she was just getting started. Mabel Kessler was having a major hissy fit. The people scattered like shrapnel. Jack stayed firm, waiting for more money quotes from Mabel, I assumed.

Jenny and Joyce made a beeline for the front door. It was my chance to corner them. "Hurry, Mabel's after you," I lied and corralled them into the large coat closet in the entryway.

"Who hired you to curse those people?" I demanded as soon as the door was closed, copying the voice I had heard Nora use so often on her multitude of kids.

"As custodians of the universal eye, we can't divulge that information," Jenny said.

"It would upset the psychical karma rainbow," Joyce agreed.

"Cut the crap!" I growled. "You're going to tell me, and you're going to tell me now. Who hired you? People are dead because of you two con artists."

"How dare you!" Jenny yelled.

"We know all about you, going around saying you talk to dead people. That's so 2002. Who do you think you're fooling?" Joyce sneered. "*I see dead people. I see dead people.* Oh, please. Amateurs like you have come and gone for years, and none of them could compete with us."

"We've been through mediums, psychics, channelers, mesmerists, scryers, and crap tons of alien abductees," Jenny said.

"And about five years of 'I see dead people,'" Joyce said.

"Damn that M. Night Shyamalan," Jenny said.

Joyce leaned forward and got in my face. "We even had Shirley MacLaine. We ran her ass out of here all the way to Santa Fe."

"Really? Shirley MacLaine?" I asked. "I loved her in *Terms of Endearment.*"

"All those people came and went," Jenny continued. "But we're still here. And all of the alien abductions, channeling, and all the rest don't matter. Because in the end, we're the only witches. Yep, we know what people around here call us. Witches."

"We're the only ones," Joyce agreed. "In other words, there's no place for you."

They flanked me on either side, trying to scare me with their witchyness. But I was done being scared. I was done being lied to, manipulated, and treated badly. "Listen," I said, punctuating my words by poking them in their chests. "The difference between me and all of you is I really did talk to dead people. And I brought a dead person to life, too. Well, that's a maybe. But anyway, none of that matters. What matters is that there's a killer out there. Or killers. In fact, I'm not convinced that you two aren't killers. But what I want to know...no, what you're going to tell me *now,* is who hired you to curse those people!"

It shouldn't have worked, but it did. They were finally ready to talk.

"I'll tell you, but then you back off," Joyce said.

"Joyce…" Jenny said, warningly.

"No more treading on our territory," Joyce continued. "No more sending spies. Yeah, we know about Nora."

"Who hired you?" I asked, again.

"Haven't you figured it out?" Jenny asked. "Margaret Marshall. The meanest bitch in Goodnight hated a lot of people. She hired us to do the curses."

PART IV: MATILDA ATTENDS THE CHILE PECKER COCK OFF, AND SHE HAS A DATE WITH THE KILLER

Potato Burglar Accuses Local Man of Murder
by Silas Miller

Shockwaves went through Goodnight today when an eyewitness came forward with an accusation of murder against Bernard Marshall. The so-called potato burglar, who has allegedly robbed and burgled at least five houses and two citizens in the past week, sent a note to Sheriff Goodnight, claiming that he saw Mr. Marshall push his mother, Margaret Marshall, off a cliff to her death.

"The investigation is ongoing, but you have to take into account the source of the accusation," Sheriff Goodnight said. "I mean, the man burgles homes with a potato."

Ms. Marshall's death was initially ruled an accident after she fell into the canyon behind her house. The new evidence, even from the dubious source, has reopened the investigation, according to sources.

When reached for a comment, Mr. Marshall insisted that he wasn't guilty. "I didn't push my mother. She wouldn't have liked that," he said.

Mr. Marshall's brother, Theodore Marshall,

reiterated his brother's innocence. "This is ridiculous. My brother won't even fish. A man who won't kill a fish won't kill his mother."

The Goodnight Gazette was not able to reach the potato burglar for a comment.

CHAPTER 13

I took Jack back to the office so that he could write the story about tomorrow's Cook-off. Silas was working on three stories at once, and I sat down at my desk and caught him up on the witches and Margaret hiring them to do the curses. I kept my promise to Amos to hold off on the information about Leonard's death.

"It sounds like it's all getting murkier," Silas told me. He kept typing while he spoke to me. "It's like the deaths were all tied, but not tied at all. Murkier than the Mississippi."

But I didn't think it was murkier. I was starting to understand that there were multiple puzzles, and yes, they were all connected. A working theory was tickling at my brain, but I still needed more information. Most importantly, I needed to know who was selling the tickets to heaven.

"Sending you the poop update story, Klee," Silas announced. He tapped on his keyboard and then he lit up a cigar.

"You want a present, boss?" he asked me with a shit-eating grin.

"What do you mean?"

"A present. A gift. A story. You want one?" He was smiling wide with the cigar in his mouth. He leaned back in his chair, making it creak loudly. I glanced over at Klee. She was busy and didn't hear Silas.

"Okay?" I said like a question. "You're not teasing me, are you? Playing a trick on me?"

"No, boss. I wouldn't do that. I'm giving you an exclusive. We need to publish it tonight. Normally, I should tell Amos about this pronto, but I like to be cutting edge. So, we're keeping this secret just for a couple more hours until we can get the paper out. You understand me, boss?"

"No."

Silas opened his desk drawer. He took something out and slammed it on my desk next to my hand. He leaned back and put his hands behind his head.

"What is that?" I asked.

"Pick it up."

I picked it up. "It's a potato. Oh my God, it's a potato. Is it *the* potato?"

"The moron dropped it at his latest burglary," Silas told me. "Cynthia Jackson's house. We're friendly, so she brought it to me. Keep looking at it."

I turned it around. "Is that…?"

"Yes."

"His name? The potato burglar's name?" I asked.

"Yes."

"The moron wrote his name on the potato? No, it can't be. You're making this up."

"Chaz Lupo."

"Chaz Lupo," I repeated. "Who's that?"

"I have no idea, but I did some searching." Silas opened his drawer again and handed me a piece of paper. "I couldn't find him, but that's his mother's name and address. Good place to start, and I know how much you like to snoop."

"Really?"

"Track him down. Write it up. Be a star. I know you can do it, boss."

He didn't have to tell me twice. I put the paper in my purse and ran out, excited that I was given my first investigative assignment. As I walked out the door,

I nearly bumped into Boone.

"Were you coming to check on me?" he asked.

"Why?"

He looked down at his feet and took a deep breath. "Because you broke my arm with a crowbar!" he yelled, raising his casted arm above his head and pointing at it with his good hand.

"I'm so sorry about that, even though you snuck up on me."

"You were skulking." We locked eyes. He had pillow marks on his cheek, and his thick hair was standing up on end. Sex hair. He was so damned sexy. It was all I could do not to run my fingers through his hair.

With everything going on, I had forgotten to feel guilty about breaking his arm. Now, he obviously wanted me to comfort him. A fantasy involving rubbing soothing oils all over his body flitted through my mind. Uh-oh. Focus, Matilda.

I patted his back. "I'm sorry you snuck up on me and I was forced to break your arm with a crowbar. I have to run out. When I come back, I'll make you more instant hot chocolate."

"Where're you going?"

"Out. I'll be back in a couple hours."

"Are you going after the witches?" he asked.

"I already did that. Now I'm on assignment." I took Boone's keys to his truck out of my purse and clutched them in my hand.

"Are those my keys?" he asked.

I put them behind my back. "Maybe."

He put his hand out, palm up. "Hand them over. I'll drive."

"But you don't know where I'm going."

"You're going somewhere where there are dead people, and you'll probably get into some life-threatening danger. Am I close?"

"You're so dramatic," I said. "This has nothing to do with dead people, and I'm not going to get into danger. I'm visiting Chaz Lupo's mother."

"Who's Chaz Lupo?"

Boone drove one-handed while I caught him up on the witches, Margaret, Bernard, Leonard, and the potato burglar. I swore him to secrecy.

"Don't worry. I'm very good at keeping secrets," he assured me.

"I noticed." I still didn't know what Boone did for a living or where he had gone for two weeks. Each time I got close to finding out, he changed the subject. As far as I could tell, his entire worldly belongings were on his body and in his truck.

Lillian Lupo lived in a tiny cottage in the middle of nowhere, about ten miles outside of Goodnight. Boone parked on the street in front of her house.

"I'm going to get as much information about Chaz as possible. That's it. Got it?" I asked Boone.

"I'll be invisible. Fly on the wall. Won't say a word."

Lillian didn't have a doorbell, so I knocked. "Coming," a woman sing-songed from inside. A minute later, she opened the door. She was a lovely little old lady, dressed in a flower-printed cotton dress and slippers. She had long gray hair pulled back in an elaborate bun. She smiled wide when she saw me, as if she had been waiting for me.

"Company! Oh, goodie. Father! Janie! Company's here," she called behind her. "Tell me, honey. Are you with the Jehovah's Witnesses or are you selling solar panels?" she asked me.

"I'm with the Goodnight Gazette. I came to ask you some questions."

"That's a first. Come on in. Do you like lemon bars? I just made a fresh batch."

Boone and I followed her inside. It was just like

Snow White's cottage, everything half-size and covered in chintz. A small bird sang in a cage, hanging from the ceiling in the corner. "This is my husband. He's shy," she said, gesturing to a man sitting on the couch. He was wearing a suit and was deep into his reading of the paper.

"Nice to meet you," Boone said to him and got no reaction. Boone shrugged at me.

We followed Lillian into the kitchen. A woman was sitting on a chair with a teacup and lemon bar in front of her on the table. "This is my sister Janie. Janie, aren't you going to say hello to our company?" Janie didn't say a thing. She was focused on her tea and lemon bar. My stomach growled. The mountain air really spiked my appetite.

Boone and I sat down at the table, and Lillian served us. "So what can I do for you, honey?"

"Actually, the Gazette is doing a story about your son, Chaz."

"Oh, isn't that nice," she said, delighted. "Is this your sweetheart, honey?" she asked, pouring tea for Boone. "He's a handsome man. Would you like sugar in your tea, handsome man, or are you sweet enough?"

"I'll take it plain. Thank you, ma'am," he said.

"Have you seen Chaz, lately? Does he live here?" I asked and took a bite of the lemon bar. My mouth puckered, and I almost spit it out. Lillian had forgotten to put sugar in the lemon bars. It was all I could do to swallow it down. Boone picked up his lemon bar, and I put my hand on his in warning and shook my head. He dropped the lemon bar back on his plate.

"Chaz hasn't lived here for quite some time. His work with the railroad takes him all over the world, you know." Lillian loved talking about Chaz. She went on and on about him as a baby, a toddler, an adolescent, and the perfect adult he had grown up to be. I assumed ninety-percent of it was lies, but even so, Lillian sure believed every word. I took copious notes.

About fifteen minutes into her monologue, when Lillian was getting more lemon bars from the refrigerator, Boone leaned over and whispered in my ear. "Don't panic."

"I'm not panicking," I whispered back.

"But you will panic. So, I'm telling you in advance not to panic."

"Why should I panic?"

"I'm debating whether to tell you. If I tell you, you're going to panic," he whispered.

"Geez, you really don't have a lot of confidence in me."

"Yes, I do. I have a lot of confidence in you that you're going to panic."

"What's going on?" I asked. "Do I have a spider on me? If I do, please get it off."

"Listen, Janie hasn't blinked once this entire time. Don't panic. Don't draw attention to yourself."

Lillian came back to the table and continued to drone on about Chaz's railroad career and how he had saved a cow. She was in her own world, content to go on and on about her son. I sneaked a peek at Janie. She was sitting rock still. She hadn't touched her lemon bar, which I didn't blame her for one bit. She hadn't touched her tea, either. Her hands were in her lap, and she was staring intently at her tea cup.

And Boone was right. She wasn't blinking.

"And he says he's starting a hedge fund," Lillian continued and went to the stove to put on more water for tea.

As soon as her back was turned, Boone hopped up and waved his hand in front of Janie's face. Then, he sat back down. "Don't panic," he whispered.

"Will you stop saying that?"

Janie still wasn't blinking. She didn't flinch when Boone waved his hand in front of her face, and she was still sitting in the same position without moving a muscle.

"Maybe she had a stroke," I whispered to Boone. He shook his head and widened his eyes at me, as if he was telling me once again not to panic.

Sheesh.

Men.

"Ms. Lupo?" I called. She turned around and smiled at me. "Ma'am, I'm worried that something might be wrong with Janie."

Lillian grew alarmed and shuffled over to her sister. She leaned over and studied Janie's face. "She looks perfectly normal to me, honey," she said.

Boone rubbed his eyes and took a deep breath.

"But she's not blinking, and she hasn't moved," I said.

"That would be pretty funny if she did," Lillian said, sitting down. "The woman's been dead for seven years."

"Don't panic," Boone whispered.

"What did you say?" I asked Lillian. She opened her mouth to speak, but I interrupted her. "On second thought, don't repeat it."

"Janie and I were best friends. Irish twins, you know," Lillian explained. "But she got the cancer. Took her real quick. One minute she was mashing potatoes, and the next minute she was gone. Snuffed out. It cost me four thousand dollars to bury her. Those people over at Goodnight Cemetery are thieves, I can tell you."

"If you buried her, then how did she get here?" I

asked.

"Lot of folks around here will do odd jobs for cash. Another lemon bar?" she asked, offering me the plate.

I shook my head. "No thanks."

"They dug her up for you?" Boone asked Lillian.

"Eight hundred dollars to embalm her. For what? So that she could just lie in the ground all lonely? Look at her. She looks better than she did when she was alive. Now she has company. I keep her up nice, don't you think? Clean outfit every day. I do her hair and makeup myself."

"Does it seem stuffy in here?" I asked, hyperventilating. "Maybe you could open a window? I'm not getting a lot of air."

"All the windows are open, honey," Lillian said.

Boone stood and yanked me up. "I think you got what you need about Chaz," he told me. "If you'll excuse us, Ms. Lupo, we've got people waiting on us."

He turned his back on Lillian, and that's when she launched forward. She was amazingly fast, considering her age and her seemingly frail body. In hindsight, though, I realized that she must have stayed strong by manhandling a corpse every day. Lillian wielded a meat tenderizer mallet in her hand, which she must have pocketed when she was making more tea.

She was fast, but Boone had lightning fast reflexes. Just as the mallet was going to land at the back of his head, he spun around and lifted his unbroken arm up in a defensive gesture. Lillian came down hard with the mallet and made contact with his arm. There was a loud *crack!*, and Boone grunted. Even in pain, he moved fast. He pushed me out of the kitchen, out of the reach of the crazy lady with the dead sister in her kitchen.

"No one's taking my family away from me!" Lillian yelled, as we ran for the door. Her husband was still sitting on the couch, totally unconcerned by the fact that his wife was trying to kill the guests.

"I can't believe she broke my other arm!" Boone yelled.

"I'm sure it's not broken," I said.

We got to the door, but it was locked. There was no way to get out. "I won't let you tell anyone! I won't let them take away my family!"

"We promise not to tell!" I yelled. We walked behind the couch and tried to reason with her, but surprise surprise, there was no reasoning with a woman who would dig up her sister and live with her corpse.

"I don't believe you!" She threw her body at Boone again, but this time he was ready. He disarmed her of her tenderizing mallet with his casted hand and tossed it in the corner.

"Listen, let's just calm down. We're not going to take Janie away," he said.

"I don't believe you!" she yelled again and pulled out another mallet from her cleavage. She had two tenderizing mallets? I guessed she had a lot of tenderizing needs.

"I'm really sorry about this, ma'am," Boone said and stepped from around the couch. With his casted arm, he punched old lady Lillian square in the face. Her mallet fell from her hand as blood spurted from her nose, and she fell to the floor like a sack of potatoes.

"You hit an old lady," I said in disbelief.

"I was saving you. Again. Dig in my pocket for my phone and call Amos," Boone instructed.

I retrieved his phone and plopped down on the couch next to Lillian's husband. He was completely unfazed by the fact that his wife was lying on the floor, bleeding. He just continued reading the paper.

I called Amos and told him to send someone over to pick up the potato burglar's mother. He said he would send Deputy Wendy Ackerman immediately. He couldn't come himself because he was busy preparing for tomorrow's Cook-off. He sounded nervous on the phone, like his whole life was on the line. I hung up. Lillian's husband was still reading the newspaper.

I pointed at him. "Look at him," I told Boone.

"Totally calm and cool."

"Don't panic," Boone said.

"What? Why?"

"Because her husband isn't blinking either."

"What?" I exclaimed.

"I'm going to tell my son on you. You'll be sorry," Lillian threatened. She managed to get herself into a sitting position, and she sounded like she had a cold, probably because her nose was broken.

"Is your husband dead, too?" I asked her.

"Our marriage has never been better since he kicked the bucket," she told me.

There was a two-hour wait at the emergency room, which gave me a good chunk of time to work on the article about the potato burglar. I wrote up all the information about Chaz's childhood and that he might work for the railroad. At the end of the article, I mentioned the part about his mother digging up his father and aunt and living with them in her house.

"I told you that it would involve dead bodies and danger," Boone said, clutching his arm to his chest in pain.

"How could I have known she was living with dead people? You act like it was my fault."

"Portal to hell, Matilda. Portal to hell."

Boone got the same doctor as the last time. "Not as gross this go around," he told Boone. "Clean break. I didn't want to throw up at all. That old lady must be dope with tenderizing meat. You want me to give you the same colored cast or you want me to mix it up with another color?"

"Sonofabitch," Boone groaned.

Boone refused the happy juice this time and just took a couple of Advils. I drove him home, tucked him into his bed, turned on the TV, and warmed up a can of tomato soup for him. Then, I went to the Gazette office and turned my story into Silas.

"What the hell?" he said reading the end of the story. "I think you buried the lead, boss."

"What does that mean?"

"It means that the potato burglar's mother lives with dead people. You don't think that's interesting?"

"I think it's gross."

"Exactly. And she broke Boone's arm with a meat tenderizer? That's gold!"

"It is?" I asked. "I thought the story was about the potato burglar."

"Those who can't do, teach," Klee commented.

"Those who can't teach, teach gym. Maybe you should teach gym, Matilda."

Ouch. Becoming a journalist was an uphill battle. It looked so easy when Dan Rather did it.

"Jack, help me out here," Silas called to the boy.

"Did you really drink tea with a dead woman?" Jack asked me.

"And I sat next to a dead guy on the couch. I'm pretty sure I have dead guy cooties on my hip."

Jack looked at my hip. "Cool!"

Silas and Jack wrote up the new stories in a hurry, and Klee got them formatted and online. I had already blabbed to Amos and Wendy Ackerman about the potato burglar's identity, and once Wendy had put Lillian in jail and called the mortuary to cart Lillian's husband and sister away to be buried again, she came to the Gazette to get the potato.

"I'm thinking of transferring to Albuquerque," she told Klee after she pocketed the potato for evidence. "They only have drug dealers and normal crime. They don't have potato crime and folks living with their dead relatives."

"Tell me about it," Klee agreed. "When's the last time a giraffe ran wild in Albuquerque? Never."

She had a point, and I wondered if I really had opened the portal to hell.

CHAPTER 14

The next morning, I took the dogs out on an extended walk in the forest because I knew it was going to be a long work day. Normally, the Gazette was closed during the weekend, but the Cook-off was the biggest event of the year in Goodnight. The entire staff of the Gazette was reporting on it. Even Klee was going to take out her reporter's notebook and interview the contestants, take pictures of the food, and report on the winners. It was an all hands on deck kind of day.

Abbott and Costello seemed to understand that something big was happening. But they were happy for the two-hour hike through the forest. When we got home, I filled up their water bowls, and they fell fast asleep, snoring contentedly.

Silas had fallen asleep in my bathtub during the

night, and it was lucky that I never sleep because I found him there when I decided to do a spring cleaning in the middle of the night. It was hard to keep the house clean when it was still a mess from the renovations that Faye started but never finished. Nevertheless, I was happy to know that my kitchen and bathroom were clean.

So, I got out the bleach and was going at it when I walked into the bathroom around three in the morning. I was shocked to find Silas there, sound asleep in the freezing water. The bubbles were long gone, and I got a big gander at his privates.

"Geez, Silas what're you doing?" I demanded, waking him. I threw a towel on him and let the water drain.

"Sorry, Matilda. I don't think I've ever written so many stories in one day. Twelve. And they were big stories, too. I'm exhausted. I guess I just fell asleep while taking a bath."

He didn't sound like himself. He was weak, and his voice wasn't the normal booming one I had grown accustomed to. He struggled to get out of the bathtub, so I helped him. He sneezed three times in a row, and I put my hand on his forehead. "You're burning up, Silas. You have a fever."

"I don't have a fever. Journalist don't get sick.

Democracy doesn't wait around while journalists get better."

"You can take my bed," I said. "I'll bring you in some Tylenol and water. Maybe you'll be better once you sleep it off."

Silas clutched my arm like a little boy trying to get comfort from his mother. "I have to cover the Cook-off, boss. If I'm not there to cover it, we'll never get it done. No offense, but I'm the only real journalist at the Gazette. There's me, a fifteen-year-old, a managing editor, and you. I need to be there. Otherwise, we'll never get all the stories done."

I tucked him into my bed. "Maybe there won't be anything big happening. Maybe we really don't need so many people reporting on it," I suggested.

"Listen, this is something you should know about, boss. The Cook-off isn't about exciting stories. It's about name dropping. It's about name dropping our advertisers' names. The Cook-off is the most popular event in town. How we handle it means how our advertising revenue is going to be for the next year. In other words, do you want to eat a steak sometime in your future, or are you going to live off peanut butter and jelly sandwiches for the rest of your life."

It was the first time that Silas had talked about the paper in a business sense instead of us saving democracy. I appreciated his candor. I did want the paper to make money. And what he said to me made total sense. This was a local event full of proud, local people. We needed to report on every aspect of it, talk about every contestant and every food dish. We had to publicize the pride that was involved with our native chiles. I totally understood what he was saying, and I was filled with a renewed sense of purpose.

"I won't let you down, Silas," I said. But he didn't hear me. He was sound asleep.

In the morning, I dressed in a straight skirt, a button-down shirt, and flats. I checked on Boone, who was doing fine despite the fact that he had a cast on both arms. He told me he was going to rest for a while and go to the Cook-off later in the day when the food was ready to be eaten.

"Amos doesn't like me hanging around until the judges taste his dish," he explained. "And Amos gets really nervous about this stuff. Wait until you see him in action."

I walked to the Plaza. It was a gorgeous morning. There wasn't a cloud in the sky, it was about sixty-eight degrees, and there was a light breeze. It was almost a sensual pleasure to be outside. Even though the organization of the Cook-off had gotten screwed up, Mabel would be in a better mood because at least the weather was cooperating.

The Plaza was already abuzz with activity. It had been closed off to traffic. The streets around the square were lined with booths. The Chile Pecker Cock Off posters had been run through with Sharpies, editing them to say Chile Pepper Cook-off. The posters weren't beautiful, but at least they were no longer R-rated.

"No! No!" I heard Mabel shout. "The tables all have to be covered. Four of them have already been poop-bombed."

I ducked into an alley before Mabel could see me and yell at me, again, for ruining Goodnight's future. With Silas's words still in my mind, I realized that I would need to have a better relationship with Mabel and Rocco, since they were big advertisers and influential people in the town. I had been trying to become a reporter, which was good, but I also needed to start thinking more like the owner of the newspaper.

The Goodnight Diner was overflowing with people. There was a huge group outside, waiting to get in. I was hoping for a leisurely breakfast before the stressful day, but there was no way I was going to get served in time.

I was about to walk by and do some early reporting and try to make up with Mabel, when Adele came out of the diner and called my name.

"Come on in here," she told me. I pushed my way through the crowd, apologizing as I went, hoping that they weren't going to kill me for butting in line.

"Don't worry about them. They don't stop eating," she complained. "The Cook-off starts in a couple hours. Can't they wait to stuff their faces?" We walked inside. It was busier than I had ever seen it. Adele had given up trying to look good, cope, or even maintain good hygiene. "Morris isn't here, of course, because of the Cook-off. I wasn't even going to open today, but Nora came by with her kids, and word got around that there were pancakes. And then this happened." She gestured to the hordes in the diner.

"Pancakes sound good," I said.

"Oh, we don't have pancakes, anymore."

She sat me at Nora's booth. Nora was sitting with five of her kids. When I sat down, Nora handed me one of her babies. She slid a bowl of applesauce toward me. "Just keep feeding him, and hopefully he won't bite you."

"Is that a thing? He bites?" I asked, trying to stay clear of the baby's mouth.

"He's a fear biter. And he gets afraid when he's hungry."

"What will you have?" Adele asked me. "It's on the house. It's the least I can do after your hospitality, and me pretty much destroying your house."

Nora blushed. "You mean, I almost destroyed her house. I'm so sorry about that, Matilda. I don't know what came over me." She took a large bunch of rope out of her diaper bag. "But the lasso practice really came in handy. I'm ready for my new job. I'm going to capture each and every giraffe and return them safe and sound and claim my bounty. Hold on a second." She threw a spoon at her son, who had climbed on a nearby table. She knocked him in the back, and he jumped down.

"The natives are growing restless," Nora said. "Take your sisters and brothers outside, she told one of her teenagers. "Don't let them do too much damage. They can chase Mabel if they want, but stay away from the cooks. Remember what happened last time. We don't want another fire."

Ten kids filed out of the diner, and we were left with only three of Nora's. "What'll you have?" Adele asked me, again. "You can have whatever you want, unless you want eggs or bread or bacon or pancakes. Damned Goodnight townspeople have cleared me out. If I put the wallpaper on the menu, they would have eaten that, too. From me to you, if someone doesn't open another restaurant or another tamale lady doesn't move to town, I'm done. I'm going to sell the diner and retire in San Diego."

"She'll never sell the diner," Nora told me when Adele left to place my order. "Her whole identity is wrapped up in this place. She hasn't gone on vacation in twenty years, and she's never even been to San Diego. I think she just mentioned it because she heard about their zoo, and everyone's got giraffes on their minds."

"About the giraffes," I started. I understood being desperate for money. I understood not wanting to go back to a dead end job that brought her no joy. But Nora wasn't thinking straight about making a living through saving giraffes. The entire town had tried to do it, and they hadn't managed to save one. Mabel had brought in so-called experts, but it was probably time to bring in real experts. People who could gather the giraffes and finally take them to the refuge in Boise. But Nora's eyes were bright with hope and the promise of financial security. So, I wasn't about to be the one to dash those hopes.

The baby on my lap finished the applesauce, and he fell fast asleep in my arms. Faye walked in, and I scooted over so she could sit next to me.

"Well, I quit the witches," she announced. "I told Norton that it would be a little longer before we could get the new UFO on the roof of the shop."

"That's a bummer," Nora said.

"What happened?" I asked.

"It turned out that those witches don't have any money," Faye said. "Thank goodness I had them pay for the supplies directly, or I'd be screwed. I'll be over at your house tomorrow, Matilda. I can't wait to get back to it. I never liked the witches' house, anyway. Totally over-the-top. But your house is the real deal. You know that Teddy Roosevelt stayed there, right?"

"He did?" I asked.

"Well, I don't really know, but don't you think if he passed through Goodnight, that would be the house he would've picked?" Faye asked. "Anyway, I'm glad I stole a bunch of supplies from those women. I'm going to redo the floors in your bathroom first."

"I was hoping you could fill in the hole in the living room," I said. "Abbott fell in it the other day, and it took me an hour to get him out."

"I forgot about that hole," Faye said.

Adele brought me my breakfast. "We didn't have what you ordered. So, I brought you the next best thing. What're your feelings about okra?"

For the second time, I left the diner hungry. Despite Nora's insistence that Adele would never sell the diner, she decided to close early when Nora, Faye, and I left. I was still holding the sleeping baby, and Nora was holding one child and holding the hand of another with her other hand.

"Yeah, that's right, binge eaters!" Adele announced to the diner. "You'll have to stuff your faces someplace else! Or better yet, give your jaws a break. They'll thank you!"

She swept the diners out with a broom. The crowd outside was upset, but she threatened them with her broom, and they scattered. "There. That's done, then," she said, and a tear ran down her cheek. "I can't meet the demands of the whole town. I've failed."

I gave her a hug. "No, you haven't. It's just a transition. You'll work it out."

"I don't think so. I mean, I fed you fried okra for breakfast."

She had a point. Something had to be done in a hurry. Adele went home to rest before the Cook-off started. Faye asked Nora and me to check out her husband Norton's booth. We found it easily. It was more or less an advertisement for his Goodnight UFOs shop. It was decorated with flying saucers and alien heads. Norton was a very large man, up and down and side to side. As far as I could tell, he loved two things: aliens and Faye.

He swept her up in his arms when we arrived,

and he planted a long, passionate kiss on her lips. "Faye and Norton have the best sex life in town," Nora said to me while Faye got kissed. "Unless you and Boone are hot and heavy. Boone had quite a reputation in high school, you know."

"He did? What kind of reputation?"

"He liked to pleasure women. You know what I mean? No girl left unhappy, if you catch my drift."

My throat went dry thinking about Boone liking to pleasure women. "We're not hot and heavy," I said. "Boone and I. We're nothing. Not even friends."

Nora barked a laugh. "Yeah right. You think that Boone spends his day driving around women just for the fun of it? That's not his style. I mean, the man broke both his arms for you. Normally, after there's broken bones, if a man hasn't seen any action, he wants nothing to do with the woman. But he's still stuck like glue to you, Matilda. Believe me, I'm an expert on these things. Thirteen kids. Remember?"

Norton stopped kissing his wife and greeted Nora and me. "What do you think of the booth?"

"You outdid yourself this year, Norton," Nora said.

"Wait until you taste my dish," he said." It's an authentic Andromedan specialty. And you know, with local green chiles. Sort of an alien-earthling fusion meal.

You want more information about it for the paper, Matilda?" he asked me with more than a little hope in his voice. It was exactly what Silas had been talking about. The event was advertisement for local businesses and townspeople. I could see how it would help rejuvenate the town and lift morale.

I took out my reporter's notebook and began to take notes about aliens' taste for spicy food and how Goodnight UFOs was on the cutting edge of alien cuisine. It wasn't easy to take notes while holding a baby, but I managed. By the time I finished interviewing Norton, the Cook-off was in high gear in the Plaza with all of the contestants busy at their booths, cooking up a storm. The atmosphere was equal parts excitement and anxiety.

Nora's husband came by with a huge stroller. He put the little children in it, freeing Nora and me to walk around. Faye decided to stay back with Norton, in order to help him. There was a lot more to the Cook-off than I had thought. Everywhere I looked, barbecues, chafing dishes, and all sorts of portable appliances we're going full steam ahead.

I made the rounds, interviewing as many people as I could. Jack was doing the same thing, and he gave me a high five when he saw me. "This is the boring part," he explained. "Once we can start eating, then it'll get good. Amos and Morris always have the best dishes, but there's a bunch else that are good, too. Have you ever had green chile fries? Best thing ever."

On the other side of the Plaza, I spotted Mabel yelling at Klee. I was relieved that she was taking the bullet instead of me. "There's Amos," Nora said, pointing. "Oh, boy, he looks bad."

Amos was sweating, and as far as I could tell, he was forgetting to breathe. We walked over to him and said hello.

"What?" he asked. "Oh yes, hello. I don't know if this is going to cut it. I hear Morris is doing a honey chile soufflé. How can I compete with that?" His voice raised in pitch. I had never seen him anything but calm and collected. It was disorienting seeing him freak out like a normal person.

"There you are." Silas came up from behind me and tapped me on the shoulder. He looked horrible, like death warmed over. "I've been looking for you. Are you doing the rounds and taking notes?"

He launched into a coughing fit, and I held my breath, trying not to catch whatever he had. I put my hand on his forehead. "Oh my God, Silas. You're still burning up. You have a terrible fever. You need to be at home in bed or maybe even the hospital."

"Does Joanne Woodward go to bed?" he

demanded.

"You mean Bob Woodward?"

"Okay. Sure. Joanne or Bob, what's the difference? Well, Bob Woodward doesn't go to bed. Does Carl Bernstein go to the hospital? Of course he doesn't! Listen to me carefully. I need to tell you what to do here. It's very important. You can't miss it. I need you to…"

Silas didn't finish the sentence. He fainted dead away, landing at Nora's feet. "Man down!" someone shouted, and a team of paramedics rushed over with a stretcher and rolled Silas onto it.

"What did he eat?" one of the paramedics asked. "Red chile scallops? Spicy Oysters Goodnight?"

"Green Chile pork balls?" the other paramedic asked.

"He didn't eat anything," I explained. "Nothing's ready yet. He started getting sick last night. He might have the flu." But it wasn't flu season. Just like it wasn't flu season for Stella. "Oh no! You need to check him for poison. Hurry, get him to the hospital."

"I haven't been poisoned," Silas moaned. "The poison that was used with Stella and Tony was slow-acting. It caused mild symptoms for days and weeks before it got bad. I haven't had anything like that. This came on suddenly. It's a virus. Do good work, boss.

Wear out your pen today."

The paramedics rushed Silas away. "The poison was slow-acting," I said out loud. The pieces to the puzzle were clicking together for me. I was getting so close, but the answer still evaded me. I left Nora to get serious with interviews. I got six of them under my belt when the smells in the Plaza grew delicious, and the food in most of the booths was ready.

Townspeople began to eat, going from one booth to another. I had chowed down on five dishes when Boone showed up. He was pretty worse for wear with his two casts on his arms, but he managed to carry a plate filled with food with one hand and a fork in the other hand.

"Did you notice that all the suspects are here?" he asked me with his mouth full. Bernard was at the Goodnight UFOs booth with his brother Ted. Next to them, Jenny and Joyce were enjoying the Andromedan specialty. And walking up to the booth was Adam Beatman with his wife.

"Holy smokes," I breathed. "They're all in one place."

"And they all love aliens, I guess," Boone said, chewing. "Damn, Morris has really outdone himself this year. I hope Amos can take him, though. Morris has won since forever. He needs to be taken down a peg."

"I knew you cared for your brother," I said. "You want him to win."

"I love him, I guess, but he's an asshole," Boone muttered.

There were a few screams, and at least a dozen people started running. I turned to see five giraffes galloping across the Plaza through the square in the center. People ran for it, but instead of running for their lives, afraid of being trampled by wildlife, they ran for their assorted ropes and nets and whatever they had created to capture the giraffes in order to get the prize money. Nora was no different.

She was just a couple booths down from me, wiping the mouths of two of her kids, when she saw the giraffes. She whipped her rope out of her purse and in her flats, ran at them, her rope turned into a lasso, swinging it over her head round and round. It was a free-for-all. Half of the people at the Cook-off started chasing the giraffes. Chile dishes went flying.

Surely this wasn't the way to change Goodnight's reputation to that of an animal-loving town.

"Yep," Boone said. "You knew this was going to happen."

"What're you talking about?" I asked him. "Nobody in their right mind could have realized that this was going to happen."

"Rocco's sure going to be pissed. I hear he spent twenty-thousand to repaint and repair the Plaza. Now it's going to have to be done again."

Behind the group of people chasing the giraffes, a large tractor roared to life. "What the hell?" I said.

Quint was driving the tractor. The people ran for their lives out of his way. Luckily, the tractor could only go about ten miles per hour, but nevertheless, Quint was determined and he wasn't going to let anything get in his way. Poor little Fifi Swan broke through the crowd in a dead run, panic on her face, as she screamed for the protection of the beloved giraffes. Somehow her seventy-year-old body managed to leap through the air and land on the tractor, where she tried to wrestle the controls away from Quint.

"Sonofabitch. Well now I've seen everything," Boone said, taking a bite of his food.

With the crowd running away, I got a good view of an old food truck parked on a side street on the other side of the Plaza. On the side of the truck was painted blue angel wings. They were faded, but I could see exactly what they were. It was the wings from the VIP Tickets to Heaven. I would've known them anywhere. Finally, I had found the scammer, the one that tied the deaths together. I knew in my heart that he was the key to finding the killer.

"I'll be right back," I told Boone. I walked quickly toward the truck, but as soon as I started toward it, its engine started up. I caught a glimpse of a man in the driver's seat as he put the truck into gear. I couldn't let him get away. I would never find him again.

The Plaza had turned into complete bedlam. The giraffes, instead of running out of the Plaza were making a tour of it, like skaters in a rink. The tractor was slow on their heels, driving at a snail's pace but with determination.

The food truck began driving down the road, and I knew I wasn't going to be able to catch it. Thinking quickly, I decided to hijack the tractor, which was cutting in front of me. It was the only way. I ran for it. Quint and Fifi were still fighting over the control of the machine. Just as I got there, Quint won the battle, tossing Fifi over the side. Luckily, Fifi fell into the arms of someone running after the giraffes. She was safe. No longer fighting for control of the tractor, Quint revved the motor. I leaped for it.

Miraculously, I got on, but I wasn't in as good of shape as a seventy-year-old, I guessed because, I wasn't totally on the top, and my feet were precariously close to the wheels. I struggled to pull myself up.

"Not another one," Quint complained. "I got

them in my sight. Why don't you people leave me alone and let me do my job?"

"In the name of the law, I'm commandeering this tractor!" I announced.

"What law?"

"I don't know, but there must be a law."

"You're not even a cop. You're just that woman from the Gazette. You can't commandeer a tractor when you're a journalist."

He was right. "You're wrong," I insisted. "We're the Fourth Estate. We're the thin line between democracy and tyranny. This tractor is essential for the continued freedom of our nation. Besides, it's not your tractor, so get off."

I finally climbed all the way to the top, and with all the strength that I could muster, I elbowed him square in the shoulder. Quint fell off the tractor. Luckily for him, he fell onto the soft grass of the square. I took command of the controls, sitting in the seat. I turned the tractor. Quint was standing up, shaking his fist at me, yelling something about doll's eyes. I didn't care. I was a woman on a mission. I aimed the tractor at the food truck.

In the truck's side view mirror, I could see the driver's expression. He knew I was after him, and he was scared. It turned out the food truck wasn't any faster than the tractor. I chased them at ten miles per hour, and he fled in his truck at about the same speed.

For some reason, he decided, instead of running in the direction outside of the Plaza, to run right for the Plaza. I wasn't deterred. I didn't care about the crowds, the giraffes, the contestants, or the booths. I was going to get him.

"Get out of my way!" I shouted at the crowd. The food truck driver was so focused on me chasing him that he wasn't watching where he was going. *Boom!* He sideswiped a booth. Then, he sideswiped another one. I saw Morris run for his life. "Stop your truck!" I called, but he was determined. At this rate, we were never going to get anywhere.

From the corner of my eye, I saw Boone walking leisurely toward us. He caught my eye and shook his head, as if to say, there she goes again. I continued my slow-speed chase after the truck, watching as it hit booth after booth. It was hard to avoid the debris, and I could feel tables crunch under the wheels of the tractor.

Just as I thought I would never catch him, Boone leisurely stepped up to the food truck at the driver's side, climbed up, punched the driver in the face, and turned off the ignition. He tossed the food truck keys outside on the ground. He opened the door and pulled the driver out.

"I didn't do it," the driver said. "I'm innocent. I didn't know those people. I had nothing to do with it. I'm innocent, I tell you."

"Keep at it," Boone said. "You sound real innocent."

"You caught him," I cheered Boone. "You did a great job."

"Matilda, turn off the tractor," Boone called.

"How do I do that?" I asked.

"You just turn it off."

I searched the tractor to see how to turn it off. "I found it!" I called, just as the tractor rear-ended the food truck with a loud crash. I stumbled off the tractor, a little shaken.

Boone walked over to me, dragging the man by his collar. "I was wrong," Boone said. "*Now* I've seen everything."

CHAPTER 15

I went from having the reputation of being a crazy woman to the woman who talked to dead people to the woman who trashed the Plaza two times.

"It withstood over five hundred years, but it couldn't stand up to you," Klee told me once the dust had cleared. The giraffes had run off happily back into the wilds of New Mexico. The tractor was still in one piece, but that couldn't be said for the old food truck or half of the Cookoff booths. Folks wandered around in shock, as if they had just survived a terrorist attack, and in a way, they had.

Despite the damage, Mabel insisted that the competition continue, and since Morris's soufflé had gotten trampled and Amos was one of the last booths standing, he finally won the blue ribbon.

"I'm so happy," Amos said, holding his first blue ribbon, as his deputies walked past him with the handcuffed VIP Ticket to Heaven salesman in tow.

Jack, Klee, and I hurried back to the Gazette and wrote an entire issue of the Gazette in record time. By the time the sun set, Klee closed up the office, and I was alone at home. I could hear Abbott howling far off in the distance. The dogs must have gone for their walk in the forest without me, and they would probably be gone for a long time. Boone had left in his truck to go somewhere. Again, he was all about the secrets, and it pissed me off.

I walked through the open courtyard to my part of the house. There were no lights on, just the light coming from the stars in the sky.

"Closer than you think," I heard a soft voice say. I squinted through the dark to see Devyn Jones. She was soaking wet, and her face was hardly more than a skull with skin wrapped tightly over it.

"Devyn," I said. "I found you in the database online. I know you ran away from your home in West Texas."

"Devyn," she repeated, as if she was tasting her name on her lips. "I'm cold. Wet. But now I'm free."

"Where are you?"

"In the water. Look for a rock shaped like

sadness, and you'll find me. Take my body back to my mother. Give her peace."

"I promise. I will," I said.

"There are others. Will you help them in time?" she asked.

"Where are they? Who's doing this to you? Tell me so I can help."

"He's closer than you think. Be careful."

And then she was gone, and I knew she would never visit me, again. Two girls had asked me for help, and I had let them both down. There were others out there somewhere, abducted, tortured, and murdered by a psychopath, and I was no closer to finding him and bringing him to justice. But if it was the last thing I did, I would catch the bastard.

At least I had caught the Ticket to Heaven guy. He was still insisting that he was innocent, but about twenty senior citizens at the Cookoff recognized him as selling them the tickets for one thousand dollars each. It would be easy to connect him to the murders.

I walked into my bedroom and turned on the lamp on my nightstand. I stripped the bed because I didn't want to catch Silas's flu. Thank goodness it was just the flu and not the poison that had killed Stella and Tony. His illness had nothing to do with that.

Two totally different things.

Different things.

Different puzzles.

"They were different things. They were connected, but they weren't connected," I breathed.

I froze in place, holding the sheets in a ball against my chest, paralyzed by the realization that I had solved the murders. I knew why each one died. Why, how, and by whom. I dropped the sheets to the floor. I needed to call Amos immediately. There was a landline in the kitchen. I left my room and walked past the bathroom and into the dark living room.

And there he was.

Waiting for me in the shadows.

The killer was in my house. He had obviously waited patiently for me to be alone, and here I was. Alone.

"I knew you would come," I lied. I had no idea. I thought I would be safe in my own home. But here he was. "You killed Margaret Marshall."

"The meanest bitch in Goodnight, although, she was always nice to me."

I nodded. It was a common refrain. The town's bully who was nice to just enough people so that she could keep bullying the ones she wanted to.

"I knew you figured it out," he continued. "The day you met me. I saw it in your eyes."

"No, I had no idea then."

"But you know now."

"Yes, I know now," I said. My voice was barely audible. My throat was constricted by fear.

"That's what I figured. You're the loose end I have to tie up. It's all been working so well up to now. I don't want to fuck it up now."

"I'm not a loose end," I assured him. "I promise I won't tell."

He smiled, obviously not believing me. "Pretty girl," he said. "Pretty girls shouldn't be smart. It ruins them. If you hadn't been so smart, we could have been an item."

"I was already married to a killer. I'm sort of off them, now. I've moved on, changed my type."

What was I saying? If I really had been smart, I would have flirted my ass off with him and tried to save my life. Now I was going to be shot through the heart or in the head, if he had good aim. Because he had a gun pointed right at me. Did I mention that?

"You're hot for the Goodnight brothers, I know," he sneered. "They never can leave the pretty women for the rest of the town. The perfect Goodnight brothers. Panty-dropping good looks. And they have money. Well, now I have money, and I have their girl.

"Who? What girl?" I asked.

"You," he said, gesturing at me with his gun.

"Uh..."

Between getting raped and getting murdered, I wasn't sure which one I would pick. But something told me that he wasn't going to give me a choice. He was going to do both. I was going to be a raped murdered girl. Damn it.

Where was Boone when I needed him? Had he gone back to the "boonies" for a few weeks, or did he go shopping for bologna and was going to walk in at any second? Either way, I couldn't count on being saved. I was going to have to save myself.

Or I was going to die.

Time. I needed time to figure out how I was going to get out of this.

"It took me a long time to realize that you were the killer," I told him. "That's because you weren't the only killer."

"What're you talking about? You mean those other old people? Yes, I didn't even know them."

"It was the perfect crime," I said. "A murder wrapped up in other murders. Different puzzles that fit together."

"Whatever," he said, shaking the gun at me.

"You know, it started with the letter from Leonard Shetland. He had worked for the witches, and he found out they were going to curse some people. He was warning the Gazette. Later I wondered if he wasn't actually warning us but rather admitting to the murders, but he died of a heart attack before Tony and Margaret died. So, he couldn't have been the killer."

"Leonard Shetland was a dork. Who the hell sends a letter these days?"

He had a point. "Jenny and Joyce, the witches, seemed to be the center of everything, the planet that everything revolved around. But it turned out that they didn't even curse those people. They said they got interrupted. So, they didn't actually do the curses they were hired for."

"This isn't very interesting," he said.

"Sorry. You might find this part interesting, though. Margaret was the one who hired them to curse those people."

"Not shocked. She was the meanest bitch in Goodnight. Remember?" He was getting impatient with me, and I knew I would have to speed it up. Jessica Fletcher was never interrupted when she solved a mystery at the end of the show. But I got no respect.

"Okay. Okay," I said. "Here's the interesting part. Margaret had no intention of cursing anybody. She hired the witches to throw the suspicion off of her. You see, Margaret was poisoning the bunch of them.

She poisoned Stella's vaginal soap and Tony's eye drops. Killed them dead. Stella died before the witches could ever do their so-called curses."

"Why did she poison them?" he asked, honestly shocked.

I shrugged. "I don't know for sure, but I don't think it really matters. I think you answered that before. She was the meanest bitch in Goodnight. She probably just didn't like them, so she offed them. The joke was on her though because she used a slow-acting poison, so she only lived to see Stella die. Tony died after Margaret did. I mean, after she was murdered."

"Holy shit."

"Yeah, it came as a surprise to me, too. But it was a matter of elimination. Eliminating all the distractions. You know, the other puzzles. I got distracted by the witches and the Tickets to Heaven, and a bunch of other stuff. But once I realized that the poisoning was separate from Margaret's murder and that Leonard died of natural causes, well, then it was easy to figure out."

I was such a liar. I had only just figured it out five minutes ago, and it wasn't confirmed for me until I was confronted with Margaret's killer in my living room.

"Margaret killed Tony and Stella," I continued.

"Cheese killed Leonard. But who killed Margaret? That was the final mystery."

He smiled, and his teeth shined.

"The obvious suspect was Bernard," I said. "The poor, sweet son who had been abused his entire life. He could have snapped easily, right? In fact, that would have been the normal thing. If I had lived with Margaret for five minutes, I would have pushed her off that cliff. So, Bernard was the obvious suspect, and I noticed that he didn't have a fear of heights at all. It would have been nothing for him to walk up along that ridge and push her off."

"Close but no cigar, then," the killer said.

"Yes. Close but no cigar," I agreed. "The potato burglar thought he saw Bernard push her to her death. But you and Bernard look like brothers. It was an easy mistake to make. And it figured that if one brother wasn't afraid of heights, then the other brother wouldn't be afraid of heights either."

"We played up there all our lives," he said. "Climbed down into the canyon. We were mountain goats."

"The abused son and the golden son. The son who could do no wrong. The son who was treated like a prince while the other son was literally tortured. It made for a perfect crime. Nobody would expect that Ted

Marshall, his mother's favorite, would have killed her. And yet you did. You brought her up to your brother's favorite spot, high up above the canyon, and you pushed her off, like she was trash that you were tired of and wanted to get rid of."

"She was trash," Ted spat, furiously. "And I might have been the favorite child, but she treated me like shit. She was a tight-fisted bitch. Sure, she was quick with the compliments for me, but you can't buy a house with compliments. You can't buy a car with compliments."

Ah, money. It was the number one motive for murder with sex being a distant second. "She didn't give you any money?"

"A pittance! She had millions, and she threw me crumbs. Crumbs! The woman had millions, and she couldn't give me a small percentage of that? Well, who's laughing now? Who has the millions now? Now, I get to live how I deserve. Now, I'm the one with the millions."

He aimed the gun at me. "Now how about we have some fun, new girl?"

I shuddered. "I'm not big on fun, Ted. I'm a huge party pooper. And not sexy. I have all kinds of body hair. That's not in fashion at all, you know."

"I don't care about body hair."

Swell, I find the only man in America who doesn't care about body hair on a woman, and it turns out that he's a rapist murderer.

"I smell, too," I continued. "I was on a tractor, and I'm pretty sure I sat in manure, or maybe it was just poop from the sky."

"Shut up."

Think quick, Matilda. Don't die. Don't get raped. As fast I could, I grabbed the thing nearest me and threw it as hard as I could at Ted. Unfortunately, the thing nearest me was a couch cushion. He swatted it away, easily.

"A cushion?" he laughed. "You're throwing cushions at me? Accept the inevitable. You're not going to escape."

I turned on my heel and ran as fast as I could. I didn't care if he was going to shoot me in the back. I was going to escape no matter what. Nobody was going to save me, so it was up to me. I heard Ted start to run after me, and then he screamed, and there was a loud crash.

I turned around just in time to see Ted disappear into the hole in the living room. He must not have seen it in the dark. As he fell in, his gun flew out of his hand and landed in a dark corner and slid along the floor until it rested under the couch.

"Help," he moaned. "My leg's broken."

I turned the light on. Ted was at the bottom of the hole, his leg bent at an unnatural angle. I had broken another man's bones. I was on a roll. "Thank you, Faye," I said out loud. "You saved me with your house renovations."

With Ted safely at the bottom of the hole with his injured leg, I walked through the living room to the kitchen to call Amos and have him come arrest Margaret's killer. I needed a drink, too. I wondered if Adele, Faye, and Nora had left me any liquor in the house. Otherwise, I would be stuck with iced tea, and I didn't think that would cut it.

Not that I wasn't happy about catching the killer. But almost getting raped and killed had me shaken. I took a deep, healing breath and reminded my body that the danger was over.

I flipped the light on in the kitchen and gasped when I saw a man sitting at my kitchen table. "You're Matilda Dare?" he asked.

I nodded slowly, afraid.

"That's what I thought. My mother gave me your name. You're a big troublemaker. You went into my mother's house and decided what? That a nice old lady was better off in prison?"

Oh my God. It was the potato burglar. He was

in my kitchen and angry about me ratting out his corpse-friendly mother. "Chaz Lupo?" I asked.

He nodded and stood. "You bitch," he spat. "You need to be shut up. Forever."

Oh, geez. Another man wanted me dead? It was an epidemic. I had always thought I was a nice person, but maybe I was wrong. Why else would so many people try to kill me?

"Can't we just be friends?" I asked.

"You put my mother in prison! You wrote about me in the paper! You put in my real name!"

"Sorry. It's part of the job."

He wasn't convinced. Sheesh. I was going to be killed by the potato burglar. What a way to go. That was going to be a real humdinger of an obituary. The potato burglar and I would be linked forever.

Swell.

I ran to the counter and lunged for a knife to fend him off, but before I could get there, there was a sound behind me. "You bitch!"

It wasn't the potato burglar.

It was Ted.

Somehow, Ted had managed to climb out of the hole in the living room. He limped into the kitchen, dragging his broken leg behind him. He had found the gun underneath the couch, and he was aiming at me.

"What the fuck?" the potato burglar said, and he went right for Ted.

It was killer against burglar. Ted after Chaz. Chaz wasn't injured, but Ted had a gun. Unfortunately for Chaz, he was focused on me, and he didn't notice that Chaz was on the attack until it was too late. Chaz ran for him and leaped, tackling him like a linebacker.

The gun went off, shooting a hole in the ceiling. I decided not to stick around. I ran like hell out of the house and into the forest. I kept running until I couldn't run anymore. Then, I sat on the forest floor. In the distance, I could hear gunfire and then finally nothing. Silence.

A moment later, I heard the jingle of my dogs' tags, as they ran toward me. They greeted me with sloppy kisses. I was so relieved to see them safe and sound. "Let's just stay here for a while," I told them. "There are bad guys at the house."

But it was dinner time, and Abbott and Costello didn't have a lot of patience for late meals. So, I followed them home because it was dark, and I was lost. But they weren't lost. A few minutes later, we were at the house.

I was surprised to find two sheriff cars in front of the house with their lights flashing. Amos and Wendy were putting Chaz and Ted into their cars in handcuffs.

"Got a call that the potato burglar was headed toward your house," Amos told me. "Are you okay?"

"Yes. No bullet holes."

"Where's asshole?" Amos asked.

"Boone took off somewhere. He didn't tell me where." And he didn't say goodbye, either.

Amos took me to the Sheriff's Department, where I gave my statement. Then, he drove me home. Adele, Nora, and Faye were waiting for me, and they stayed with me for the night. There's nothing better than friends.

CHAPTER 16

Faye had been working on my house for four days straight. Mostly she was fixing the damage from the gunshots, the lasso practice, and the renovations she had started and but didn't finish. First thing she did was fix the hole in the living room, which had saved my life.

Adele was still frazzled, and she was talking more and more about selling the diner and moving to San Diego. Meanwhile, Nora was despondent. The bank refused to take her back, and now she was completely unemployed without any employment prospects, especially since there hadn't been any sign of the giraffes since the Cook-off.

Fifi had even left town, and Quint had decided to go back to retirement. It was almost as if everyone had given up on ever finding the giraffes and returning them to the sanctuary. The poop falling from the sky had also ended. Nobody had been poop-bombed since the Cook-off.

On Wednesday, Amos came to the house. He was in a fabulous mood, and his blue ribbon was hanging from his rear view mirror. I had asked him to help me find Devyn's body, and it took him until then to get around to it. Since Saturday, he had wrapped up all of the arrests. He also got most of the money returned to the senior citizens who had purchased VIP Tickets to Heaven. The Plaza was undergoing another paint job, and basically everything was getting back to normal in Goodnight. Searching for a possible dead girl who had spoken to me was further down on the totem pole in Amos's To Do list.

I hopped up in Amos's SUV, and we drove off. "I think I know where to go," he told me. "A rock shaped like sadness could be up north at the Snake River. There's a bunch of boulders there, and it's a good place to dump a body."

We drove out to the river. It was a gorgeous spot. Very isolated and wild. A cold wind blew.

"Autumn is coming," Amos said. "Most beautiful time of the year in Goodnight. Look over there. Does that boulder look like sadness?"

There were three large boulders in the middle of

the river. One of them had two indentations near the top, and when the spray of water hit the rock, it looked eyes were crying.

"Yes! Oh my goodness, how did you ever find it?"

"Lived here my whole life," Amos said. "When Boone and I were eight, we went camping and exploring on our own for a solid week."

"Your mom let you do that when you were eight?"

"My mother used to tame wild horses. She had an understanding of how to treat wild creatures."

"By letting them free?" I asked.

"By letting them believe they're free. I'm pretty sure she followed us out into the wild, watching us from afar." Amos stared intently at the boulder and took a deep breath. "I see her blond hair. Oh, Matilda. I'm so sorry for doubting you."

He waded into the river, and I watched from the shore. He stopped at the boulders and began to heave something from between them. It was a body, bloated and almost unrecognizable, but it was mostly preserved in the cold water, and it had long blond hair.

"Oh no," I said, even though it wasn't a surprise. "Poor girl. She didn't deserve this. She was so young. She had so much life left to live."

Amos made some calls in his car and then came back. "I'll bet my retirement that the psycho dumped her a little upriver, and then she got caught here. Lucky for us. Not lucky for him. I'm going up there to see if I can catch any forensic evidence. It hasn't rained, so I'm hopeful."

He took a plastic briefcase out of his trunk and carried it upriver, while I stayed with the body. I was careful not to touch her, but I did look at her, trying to find some clues. Her body was so bloated and distorted that I couldn't see anything that would point to her killer.

Amos returned after a few minutes. "Footprints," he said. "Size eleven, I'm guessing."

Deputy Adam Beatman arrived in his car, and the coroner was behind him. Adam shook my hand when he got out of his car. "Thank you for saving me," he told me. "I owe you one for clearing my name." It was my first thank you for capturing a killer, and it made me feel giddy.

The coroner went over the body with Amos when a black SUV arrived and parked behind the coroner's car. "Feds," Adam told me. "I guess that means we have a serial killer."

I shuddered.

Three men left the black SUV. They wore suits

and sunglasses, just like in the movies. "Hey guys, what can we do for you?" Adam asked them.

"You found a second girl?" one of the feds asked.

"Boss did," Adam said. "Are you fellas taking this over?"

"Tandem investigation. Maybe we can help each other out. Our resources and your familiarity with the area."

Adam nodded and called Amos over. They talked among themselves, and I noticed that Amos left me out of the conversation. I mean, he didn't mention me. Didn't mention that I spoke to dead girls. Didn't mention that I knew her name.

It wasn't lost on me that Amos was protecting me. The FBI probably didn't believe in the ability to talk to the dead. And because of that, I would become suspect number one. So, it was just the facts, ma'am. Amos agreed to hand over the body and scene of the crime to them.

He shot me a look, which I took to mean that the FBI may have the forensics, but he had me. The woman who could talk to the dead.

After the scene was secured, Amos offered to drive me home. Before we left, I asked one of the feds about the poop from the sky. "Do you guys know where that was coming from?"

"Sorry ma'am. That's classified. Way above your pay grade."

"Joke's on you," I said. "I don't have a pay grade."

It was the truth. I was poorer than I ever was. If I was cut, I would bleed peanut butter and jelly. My stomach growled. "Can you drop me off at the diner?" I asked Amos. "I'm going to try again to get a meal."

"I hate that there's a serial killer in my town," he said. "We have quirky townsfolk, sure. We have runaway giraffes, sure. But serial killers? No. Never. It makes me fighting mad."

He dropped me off at the diner and went back to talk more with the feds. Silas was standing outside the diner. His flu had turned out to be the twenty-four-hour kind. I gave him the rundown about the girl.

"Holy cow, since you've moved here, things have really gotten exciting in our small town," Silas said.

"Are you going into the diner to eat?" I asked.

"I already tried. I never thought I'd see the day, but I think Adele is really going to sell. She just can't take it. Someone needs to pick up the slack soon, or she's a goner. What am I seeing?"

I turned around. A herd of giraffes—all of them, as far as I could tell—were galloping into the Plaza, but instead of running wild, they seemed to be running in formation. And then I saw why. Behind them, Boone was riding a horse, cracking a whip over his head, corralling the giraffes without hurting them.

"It's the Man from Snowy River," I breathed. My hormones went into overdrive. Boone rode his horse with one hand, a master of the horse and master of the whip. He was tall in the saddle, his back straight, his skin tanned. He was a hubba hubba, hotter than hell, sexiest man alive giraffe herder. I wanted him bad.

The giraffes stopped in the square, seemingly content to stay there. Rocco came running, ecstatic that his giraffes had returned safely. Men came out of nowhere, gathering the metal barriers that had been used for the Cook-off to encircle the giraffes. They were corralled.

Boone hopped off his horse and walked it over to me. "Hey there, Matilda. Hey, Silas," he said. Adele and most of the diners walked out to see Boone's miracle. Nora was with them, and two of her children ran to the square to pet the giraffes.

"How did you do it?" Rocco asked, running toward us.

"It wasn't hard," Boone said. "I don't know why no one could catch them before. Sweet animals. Like cows, but they smell better."

"Thank you, thank you, thank you," Rocco gushed. "Our town is saved. I'll cut you a check."

"Make it out to Nora Montana," Boone said.

"Really?" Nora asked, shocked.

"Really?" I asked, too.

"Yes. I thought the money could go toward buying the old food truck."

"The one that I crashed into?" I asked.

We all looked over at the spot across the Plaza where the food truck remained after I crashed into it with the tractor.

"That's the one. I figure that sixty thousand dollars is enough to fix it up and get started with Nora's own food truck business. I always thought you made better tamales than the tamale lady, anyway," Boone told Nora. "And that way, Adele can get some relief, too."

Nora started to cry, and Adele cried, too. "I'll help you," Adele told Nora and gave her a big hug. "Now I don't have to move to San Diego."

"And I bet I can fit at least three kids in the back of the truck while I work," Nora said. "This is the best gift I've ever gotten. Oh, Boone, you're going to eat free tamales and burritos for the rest of your life."

They hugged Boone and went off to check out the truck to determine all the wonderful possibilities it could offer.

Boone put his arm around my waist and walked me a little ways away from the diner. His horse followed us.

"That was a very nice thing you did," I told him.

He arched an eyebrow. "I like Nora, but I did it because you love her."

"Oh," I breathed.

He put his casted arms around me and pulled me in close. He lowered his head to me. "I'm a paleontologist," he whispered. "A dinosaur hunter. And I've found the dinosaur that survived."

Then, he kissed me. His lips pressed firm against mine. He urged my mouth open, and his tongue explored my mouth, making me crazy with desire and my body flood with heat. I wrapped my arms around him, too. My fingers danced along the long muscles of his back. Even though he was much taller than I was, our bodies fit together, and as we kissed and kissed and kissed and kissed, I wondered if they would fit together horizontally, too.

Be sure to watch for the next installment of the Goodnight Mysteries: **Jurassic Dark**. Sign up for my newsletter to be the first to know when it's released.

http://elisesax.com/mailing-list.php

Would you like to see how it all began? Read **An Affair to Dismember**, the first book in the Matchmaker Mysteries.

ABOUT THE AUTHOR

Elise Sax writes hilarious happy endings. She worked as a journalist, mostly in Paris, France for many years but always wanted to write fiction. Finally, she decided to go for her dream and write a novel. She was thrilled when *An Affair to Dismember*, the first in the *Matchmaker Mysteries* series, was sold at auction.

Elise is an overwhelmed single mother of two boys in Southern California. She's an avid traveler, a swing dancer, an occasional piano player, and an online shopping junkie.

Friend her on Facebook: facebook.com/ei.sax.9
Send her an email: elisesax@gmail.com
You can also visit her website: elisesax.com
And sign up for her newsletter to know about new releases and sales: elisesax.com/mailing-list.php
Or tweet at her: @theelisesax

Made in the USA
Middletown, DE
14 March 2019